BR

BIG

BREAKING BIG

Penny Draper

ORCA BOOK PUBLISHERS

Library and Archives Canada Cataloguing in Publication

Draper, Penny, 1957–, author
Breaking big / Penny Draper.
(Orca limelights)

Issued in print and electronic formats.
ISBN 978-1-4598-0923-9 (paperback).—ISBN 978-1-4598-0924-6 (pdf).—
ISBN 978-1-4598-0925-3 (epub)

I. Title. II. Series: Orca limelights
PS8607.R36B74 2016   jc813'.6   C2015-904498-7
                    C2015-904499-5

First published in the United States, 2016
Library of Congress Control Number: 2015946191

Summary: When another ballet dancer's injury lands him a major role,
mischief-loving Robin must face his friends' jealousy and the biggest
challenge of his dance career in this novel for teens.

*Orca Book Publishers is dedicated to preserving the environment and has
printed this book on Forest Stewardship Council® certified paper.*

Orca Book Publishers gratefully acknowledges the support for
its publishing programs provided by the following agencies:
the Government of Canada through the Canada Book Fund and the
Canada Council for the Arts, and the Province of British Columbia
through the BC Arts Council and the Book Publishing Tax Credit.

Cover design by Rachel Page
Cover photography by Corbis

ORCA BOOK PUBLISHERS
www.orcabook.com

Printed and bound in Canada.

19 18 17 16 • 4 3 2 1

To Clinton, who dared to dream big

One

"Hurry up, enough already!"

I add the final touches. All the pointe shoes are braided together and hanging from the ceiling, loose leotards and leggings are stuffed into the Lost and Found, and Sybille and Johanna's lockers are stacked. I set Jeremy's rat cage on a bench and put all the hairbrushes inside it—along with Ratinski the rat. He's sure going to have fun for the next hour or so! Then a quick swipe of Vaseline on the combination locks. There's no time to do anything else. I check to make sure the door is locked from the inside, then climb out the window onto Cam's shoulders. He's laughing so hard I think he's going to drop me.

"What took you so long?" croaks Jeremy in a whisper as I drop down to the ground and we hoof it away from the girls' locker room. "I was sure we were going to get caught!"

"I am an *artiste*," I reply loftily, waggling my fingers. "Best prankster this side of the Rockies."

"The girls are going to go ballistic," laughs Cam. "I can't wait to see Miss High-and-Mighty's face!"

"Ah, yes, the lovely Odette, late for class." I pretend to swoon. "The whole world may come to an end!"

Jeremy checks the time. "We need to get to class."

"Yeah, we better be warming up when Mr. Colson arrives, so he won't suspect anything," I agree.

"Oh, come on, Rob, get real," Cam punches me in the arm. "Of course he'll suspect you!"

As we walk over to the rehearsal studio, I think about that. Yeah, it's probably true. I do have a rep for this sort of thing. But honestly, the dancers at this school are so intense. I mean, ballet is great and all, but can't everybody loosen up? I've been at the Premier Dance School for three years now, and some of these elite dancers can be real stiffs. Yeah, yeah, I know, ballet is all proper and solemn, and there are a lot of rules, but do you have to follow them *all* the time? I see absolutely no reason why dancers can't crack a smile from time to time, so I've decided to make it my mission.

It's 9:46 AM. We're first in the studio, as planned. We're well into our warm-up when Mr. Colson arrives and looks around.

"Where are the ladies?" he asks.

We shrug our shoulders and keep warming up. Ten o'clock comes and goes, but no girls. Mr. Colson's getting antsy. At exactly 10:22 the girls come roaring into class, shoe ribbons trailing, hair in loose ponytails instead of tight buns, warm-ups thrown over shoulders. Perfect! Even the marvelous Odette has a loose bobby pin.

Charis is hopping on one foot as she tries to put on a shoe. "Sorry, Mr. Colson. We couldn't get into our dressing room—the door was locked!"

All eyes in the room turn to me. "What?" I ask innocently. Cam and Jeremy are doing face contortions, they're trying so hard not to laugh. We'll need to work on that. I used to practice innocent looks in the mirror. I can coach them.

"Steady on, ladies," says Mr. Colson. "Take a minute, catch your breath, and pull yourselves together. And get that hair fixed! If Miss Amelia comes in and sees all that hair flying about, there will be consequences!" Then he turns to the rest of us.

"Men, the ladies will need some time to warm up, which is an opportunity for you. I know we don't usually begin with the double tour en l'air, but let's not waste the chance." I get the evil eye. "Robin. Perhaps you could start."

Shoot. This wasn't supposed to happen. I hate the double tour. Every male ballet dancer has to be able to do one. It's the grand finale, the showy finish, the most important move of the whole dance for a guy. And I can't do it. I mean, I can do everything else. Of all the guys in the pre-professional program, I'm one of the best. And that's not bragging—it's fact. But I can't do a double tour.

Odette is smirking as I take my place in the middle of the room. I ignore her. *I am a rocket. I can fly.*

And I try to believe it as I go through the move in my head: feet in fifth position, plié, then fly straight up, rotating as I go. Twice. I take a deep breath and start the prep. Angling my right foot ninety degrees and my left ninety degrees in the opposite direction, I push my feet together, left heel touching right toe, right toe touching left heel. I bend my knees, energy shoots from my toes upward, and I'm flying, I'm turning...

"Robin, I've told you again and again. Keep your hips level! If your weight isn't the same on both feet, you'll shoot sideways, not straight up." Mr. Colson sighs. "You can't fit the turns in if you're sideways. Again."

And again, and again. *Okay, I get that I'm being punished. But enough already!*

"Robin, that's enough for today—you're going to hurt yourself." *Finally.* The girls are ready, and we all go to the barre. My thighs are on fire for the rest of the class. Maybe I should have listened to my dad and become a soccer player. It would have been easier than ballet school.

"All right, everyone, remember that class is canceled this afternoon. The company is back from their tour, and they'll need the large studio to prepare for tonight's fundraiser. Dinner will be served early, and you are all to meet in the lobby by six o'clock to hand out donor forms and meet with patrons. Dress presentably. Thank you very much."

Jeremy bumps me on the way out of class. "Ya gotta breathe when you jump, man! You look like a blocked pipe ready to blow!"

I shove him back. "Hmm. Could be messy."

Cam catches up. "Yeah, I always knew you were full of it!"

Jeremy busts up laughing.

I lunge at Cam, who fakes a double tour to get out of the way. Then Charis gives me a shoulder punch while I'm off-balance.

"Hey!" I shout.

"Serves you right!" she says. "That stupid rat destroyed my hairbrush!"

"As if a brush could help that rat's nest you call hair," Odette sneers as she rolls her eyes and pushes out the door. We all ignore her.

"Come on, it was just a joke," I say.

"A joke? Do you see me laughing?" says Mavis. "I got Vaseline all over my leotard. It'll never come out!"

"Okay, I'm sorry," I say. "I'm sorry!"

Charis glares at me, but then—wait for it—yeah, I get a bit of a smile. I can always count on Charis.

"You make me crazy, Robin Goodman," she says, grinning at me. "You know I hate you?"

"Nah, you love me. You all love me."

Mavis gives me another punch for that, but she's smiling too. Mission accomplished. Except, of course, for odious Odette, but she's beyond hope.

"Hey, look!" interrupts Jeremy. "There they are."

We stop horsing around. All of us, even Odette, watch a bunch of the company dancers take over the studio. They've been on tour for a month, and it's like all the energy goes out of this place when they're away. This is what we're here for, after all. To learn to be like them. To study and practice and totally wreck our bodies, all for the chance to take our place onstage and dance. As we watch, I'm looking for Noah Grayson. He's a principal. In a dance company, that's what the stars are called, the ones who get all the lead roles. Noah's the most amazing athlete I've ever seen, even if at thirty-five he's kind of old. But he isn't there.

"There's Rick Mathews!" Sybille sighs dreamily. She leans closer to the studio window to get a better look. "Don't you think he's amazing?"

Cam snorts.

"Sybille, I thought you were in love with Daniel," Johanna says, pointing to a company dancer warming up in torn green sweats. "Or was that last week?"

"Dreamboat? Isn't that what you called him?" Charis asks sweetly.

Cam, Jeremy and I are all laughing now.

"Eww. Of course not," replies Sybille. "Didn't you hear how he messed up on the tour? How could anybody fall for a guy who misses his entrance cue?"

Unbelievable. It's true that ballet dancers live in kind of a weird world, but only we can be so socially backward as to fall out of infatuation because of a missed cue.

"When I get into the company, I'm counting on girls loving me for my body, not my entrance cues," I state firmly.

Sybille turns away from the window and gives my body a long, slow look. "Good luck with that," she says. Charis bursts out laughing.

Very funny.

"As if Rick Mathews would ever look at you, Sybille," says Odette nastily. "You still don't get that students are invisible to the company?"

"I can dream, can't I?"

"Leave her alone, Odette," Charis says.

Odette shrugs her shoulders. "I'm only trying to be realistic."

"No, you're a downer, that's what you are," Sybille says.

"Don't pay any attention to her," says Charis, matching Odette glare for glare. "I never do."

Two

We watch the rehearsal for a while, until Jeremy says, "Let's get out of here. We've got an afternoon off. What do you want to do?"

Cam's eyes light up. "Let's go skateboarding!"

We knock fists. He's unbelievable on a skateboard. Half my size, Cam is kind of like a rubber ball, flexible and fast. He's only marking time here at the ballet school. What he really wants is to be an aerial-silk performer in the circus, and dance is kind of like cross-training for him. Jeremy's different. He comes from a ballet family. Everybody in his family dances, so it's like his birthright or something.

Me? I don't have to dance, I just want to. It was a tough sell in my family at first, considering

I have two older brothers who are heavy into sports. But Mom's the law in our house, and she was on my side right from the day I announced I wanted to dance. It's all her fault anyway, since she was the one who dragged us boys to see *The Nutcracker* one Christmas. She thought we needed to get cultured. After that, my brothers teased me about being a girl, but it didn't last long. Turns out that even though I'm the youngest *and* a "sissy dancer," I'm the strongest. Now that I can take either one of them, nobody's laughing. Dancing makes me feel strong. Not Incredible Hulk strong, like my football-star brothers. More like Superman strong, as if I could leap off tall buildings. What could be cooler? And anyway, I'm good at it. Even my brothers get that.

"Skateboarding? Not me," says Jeremy. "My mom will kill me if I break my ankle."

Well, he's right about that. Jeremy's mom is kind of fierce, like a grown-up Odette. Poor guy. I can't even imagine it.

"Let's go downtown and act like real people for a change. Get a coffee. Go to a store or something," says Charis.

"Oh yeah, shopping. I'm so excited! Let's go, boys!" I say in a high falsetto voice. "You're kidding me, right? Waste an afternoon on *shopping*?"

"Then how about the movies?" Sybille suggests. "I love the movies!"

"Yeah, why not?" agrees Jeremy quickly.

Really? The movies? Then I get it. Jeremy, as usual, is looking like a basset hound as he casts his sad, lovesick eyes Sybille's way. It's unbelievable that a girl who so badly wants to be in love can never see the guy right in front of her. The same guy who manhandles her body, touches her in very personal places and sees her half naked day in and day out. I don't get it, but then, I don't get Jeremy on this one either. Sybille's just plain flaky. But a friend's a friend, so the movies it is. I'll do a little maneuvering to make sure Jeremy gets to sit next to her. Give them a dark theater, and who knows what might happen? Cam clearly knows what I'm thinking and looks my way, shaking his head. Jer is useless when it comes to women.

"Well, have fun, kiddies," Odette calls over her shoulder as she sweeps off down the hall. "Charis, I know you and your little friends need to have your playtime."

Charis responds by staring heavenward as if asking for patience.

We leave the school grounds so seldom it's almost an adventure to take the bus. It's crowded, so we have to stand. The swaying of the bus feels interesting. I close my eyes and sway with it, feeling the transfer of weight and the way my core takes over when the bus turns a corner. I pick up the motion in my shoulders, exaggerate it a bit, then...

Charis digs me in the ribs. "Try to act normal," she hisses.

"Hey!" My eyes snap open. "What about him?" I nod to where Cam is standing, holding on to a pole and humming. Loudly.

"He's got headphones on—people will think he's singing to the music. You...you look weird. And you're tall. You stand out more."

"Sorry for living," I drawl.

It's true that when we're out in the real world, we dancers look a little odd, especially when we walk. My brothers remind me of this regularly. They call it the duck walk. Dancers tend to walk as if they're in first position—hips turned out, heels together, toes out. But I don't think we look like ducks. I prefer to think we're noticeable because we're the only people who are standing up straight.

Piling off the bus, we argue about which movie to see, but Cam and I know Jer is going to pick whatever Sybille wants, so we'll be outnumbered. Whatever. Mavis slows as we pass the popcorn stand, and Johanna and Charis have to grab her by the arms and steer her past the temptation. Popcorn bloats. We shuffle into the theater, and I try, I really do, but in the end, all the maneuvering in the world can't help Jeremy if he refuses to be helped. He ends up sitting behind, not beside, Sybille.

"Why don't you just tell her you like her?" I whisper as the lights dim.

"And be shot down?" he replies. "The girls will all gang up on me."

Unfortunately, he's right about that. They're so close, dating one would be like dating them all, which is a really good reason not to date anybody.

On the way home, we get off the bus a couple of stops before the school to check out the skate park. Cam can hardly bear to watch without getting antsy, so in no time he's negotiated the loan of a board. We're not his only cheering section. Pretty much everybody stops to watch. He's that good.

"Thanks, man," Cam says as he hands back the board. "I needed that."

"Honestly, what are you doing in ballet school?" I have to ask.

"Apparently, I need to improve my flexibility and body awareness," he replies with a grin. "At least, that's what my coach said. Jer's my model for that. And if I'm going to fly through the air while dangling from an itty-bitty piece of fabric, I have to work on my confidence. That's what you're for. So when I'm a circus star, you can say it's all because of you."

*   *   *

Back at school, it's fish and veggies for dinner in the cafeteria. Mavis gets there first and nails down our table. She waves to show us where she is, and we all settle in with our trays.

"Rumor has it there's going to be a big announcement tonight at the gala. I bet they're going to tell us what the next production will be," says Charis. "I'm taking bets, a dollar a guess. Who's in?"

"I heard that the artistic director wants to do something modern, maybe even something completely new," replies Mavis. "No way we can guess that."

"Your guess can be 'new and modern.' You're in for a dollar. Who else?"

"Something with props," guesses Cam. "Props are all the rage. Remember the company that danced with crutches and canes and wheelchairs?"

Sybille frowns. "But our company is pretty traditional. Surely they'll do a story ballet. Maybe *Giselle*?"

"I guess *Sleeping Beauty*," says Johanna.

"*Peter Pan.*"

"*Coppélia.*"

It turns out they're all wrong.

Three

The pre-professional program at the Premier Dance School is one of the best in the country. You have to audition to get in, and it's not only talent the adjudicators are looking for. It's potential. You have to have the right body and the right attitude as well as the right moves. And even if you get in, you're not actually in. The first audition is for summer school. They pick kids from right across the country to come to the school for four weeks in July to live, eat and train with each other. It's like every day is an audition. At the end of the four weeks, you have to go home and wait for a letter. Only the very best get picked to return in September and stay for the whole school year. The stress is mind-numbing.

I got the letter three years ago. When it came, I couldn't open it. I took it to my room, laid it on my bed and sat there looking at it. I could hear Mom pacing back and forth in the kitchen, pretending even harder than I was that getting into Premier didn't matter. She knew how much I wanted it. I finally opened it only because I could hear my dad and my brothers throwing a foot-ball around in the backyard. They never do that. They always go to the high-school playing field, because my brothers throw so well they need a huge field to practice in. They were hanging out, waiting for me to open the letter. Everybody was rooting for me, so I opened it, and here I am. Some days I still can't believe it.

We all live at the school. It's three to a room, and Cam, Jer and I always room together. We get bused to a regular public school most mornings for math, science and all that other useless stuff, but at least we only have to do half days. Then it's back to our real school to work on the important stuff—dance.

All of us are on full scholarship, so part of the deal is making nice with patrons who donate the money to pay our room and board. It's a really great school, so we don't mind too much. Although it feels kind of weird when old ladies dressed in sequins come over to meet us, then talk about our bodies right in front of us. *Thighs like that, Marjorie, this strapping young man is going to be a great jumper, don't you think?* Yech. They do it with the girls too. It takes some getting used to.

So we're all hanging out near the doors at the back of the theater, ready to hand out donation forms, when the announcement comes. At first there is total silence. Then gasps and groans. The next production is going to be *A Midsummer Night's Dream*. And the reason for this nice, safe, traditional choice? Principal dancer Noah Grayson has a tear in his Achilles tendon. He's out for months. At his age, maybe forever.

Jeremy's gone absolutely white. I'd laugh at the look on his face, except this isn't funny. "Cam, you can't ever go skateboarding again! Look what can happen!"

Cam frowns. "Jer, Noah wasn't skateboarding. That's crazy. They said he tore it coming out of a jump."

"Probably a double tour," I mutter under my breath.

"It doesn't matter how he did it," Jeremy says. "This could absolutely finish his career!"

"Calm yourself, Jeremy," says Mavis, patting him on the back. "It's kind of tragic, all right, but it's not *your* leg. I wonder who'll dance the lead now that Noah can't do it."

That is so the right thing to say to Jeremy, and I grin at Mavis. With Jer's family background, we depend on him to get us the inside story on stuff like this. The company dancers are a pretty tight group, but all of them are going to start competing for the top job. It's a given.

"Hey, Jer, can you talk to your mom?" I ask. "I bet she knows who will get the role."

"On it," he promises.

"Hey," says Charis. "Nobody won the bet. What say we order pizza with the money?"

* * *

Next morning the halls are crazy with rumors. Everybody's got a theory, but nobody's got any answers, not even Jeremy's mom. The girls have made these stupid get-well cards for Noah, which they make everybody sign before class.

"Guess I shouldn't say, *Break a leg*, huh?" I whisper to the guys. Cam snorts.

We warm up and are about halfway through our barre exercises when Miss Amelia, the director of the school, comes into the studio. We keep doing battement tendus while she talks to Mr. Colson. Devant, à la seconde, derrière—front, side, back. Balancing on one foot while we slide the other toe to the front, the side and the back, stretching our insteps over and over again. Then Mr. Colson signals the pianist to stop playing and looks straight at me.

"Robin, will you please go with Miss Amelia?" he asks.

I sigh. I guess it was too much to expect odious Odette to keep quiet about why she was late for class. But the situation gets a little more intense when Mr. Colson hands the class over to the rehearsal assistant and comes with us. None of us say a word as we walk down the hall toward the office, and I'm starting to get a little nervous. It was just a joke.

Miss Amelia opens her office door and waves us in. Bellamy Acton, the artistic director of the company, is waiting for us. *Whoa.* I've never

"It would be an honor, Mr. Acton," I say before he can change his mind. Then a horrible thought crosses my mind. "Ah, this isn't a joke, is it?"

"In retaliation for something you've done?" Another grin from Mr. Acton. "Hardly," he adds drily. "My pranking days are over."

It's amazing that another ballet dancer even had pranking days. I'm going to like working with Mr. Acton. Everybody's smiling now, and there are papers to sign, and I get a rehearsal schedule and a lecture about hard work and discipline. *Yeah, yeah, I get it.* I'm going to understudy Puck! I pretty much fly out the door and race back to class.

"So how much trouble are you in this time?" Odette says with a sneer. Cam and Jeremy look concerned, and even Charis seems a little worried.

"I'm going to understudy Puck!" I whoop.

Their faces go blank. And then I see the news start to seep in, and Cam is the first to react. He starts jumping up and down and then he grabs my hands, and I'm jumping up and down too.

"Way to go!" he cheers.

Jeremy doesn't cheer. He just stands there, looking dazed. "They asked *you*?" he finally says.

What the heck? "Is that such a crazy idea?"

"Well, it's kind of unexpected, don't you think?" he replies.

"What are you trying to say?"

"Nothing, man." Jeremy shakes my hand stiffly. "Ah, congratulations, Rob."

The girls all look a little shocked—except for Odette, who's furious. "Boys get all the luck," she says angrily. "And you? No way you deserve it." Then she stalks out of the studio, leaving behind an uncomfortable silence.

"Ah, really, it's great, Rob," says Charis finally. "We're happy for you, aren't we?" She looks around at the others.

"Oh yeah, of course," they chime in.

"Way to be enthusiastic," I grumble. "Look, maybe there'll be more understudy parts." The others brighten a little at the thought. "And if not, at least one of us can uphold the reputation of the Premier Dance School!" I add cheerfully.

"That's what we're worried about," Mavis says. She pauses, then shoots a small grin my way. She means it as a joke. At least, I think she does.

Four

Jeremy, Cam and I head to the change room. Jeremy has gone all quiet, but he does that sometimes. Cam is chattering mindlessly, eyes darting back and forth between Jer and me.

Then Jeremy cuts into Cam's babble. "Are you sure you're ready for this, Rob? It's a big step, and you don't have any experience working with the company."

Is he kidding? "Well, duh. This is how I'm going to *get* some experience! It's not like anybody else from our class has danced with the company."

"Actually, I have," he replies. "I played one of the little fairies when I was a kid. Did you know Puck's solo ends with a double tour? Are you going to be able to do it?"

"Geez, Jer, they wouldn't have picked me if they didn't think I was ready." I don't really want to think about the double tour.

"All they know is that you've got potential. Nobody knows if you're ready!"

"What are you getting at, Jer?" I ask. I'm angry now. "You want me to say, *No, I won't do it*? Maybe say you should do it instead? I never pegged you as the jealous type."

"Get over yourself, Rob! I'm not jealous. I'm just looking out for you," he retorts. "You should really think about this. If you blow it, it could be the end for you with the company."

"And the beginning for you?" I shoot back.

"Give me a break!" Jeremy's shouting now, and Cam looks scared. "We're friends! I didn't mean that I wanted the part."

I jam my stuff into my locker and head for the door. "Well, thanks for the great advice. And the support and encouragement." I make sure to slam the door on my way out. I can't believe him. I'm not stupid. I know that being an understudy is going to be hard, but nobody—*nobody*—says no when a chance like this comes up. You'd be crazy to refuse. I was counting on the guys to help me through it—help me practice, maybe—because the company dancers aren't going to pay me much attention. But that doesn't look likely, not with them acting all put out because I was the one who got the break.

Unless, of course, I can bring them around. Why can't we all get something out of this? They help me, and I bring back what I learn from the company?

It sounds completely reasonable to me.

*   *   *

I'm the last one to the cafeteria for lunch, and there's hardly any room left at our table, so I have to push in. Did they forget I was coming? "Somebody must be putting on the pounds!" I joke as I make everybody shift over.

Nobody laughs. "You're going to be the only student understudy," reports Jeremy. "I checked."

"Oh. Wow." What else can I say?

"So it's only you representing the school," adds Johanna. "Mavis is right. That's a scary thought!" Everybody laughs, although I don't know if it was meant to be funny.

"So maybe you guys could help me practice?" I ask. "Mr. Acton won't want to spend much time with the understudies."

There's an awkward silence. Charis finally speaks up. "That probably won't work," she says. "Mr. Acton won't want us sticking our noses into it. We might say the wrong thing and mess you up." The others nod in agreement. "Don't worry—you'll be fine."

Conversation around the table starts up again. Sybille goes back to mooning over Rick, Mavis reminds her that company members can't fraternize with students, Johanna makes a rude comment about some girl's weight (why do they laugh when *she* says it?), Cam tells Jer about this new song he's downloaded, but of course Jer isn't listening because he's all basset hound over Sybille, and everything is the same as it usually is, except that I'm invisible. I really, really didn't expect this.

I inhale the bean salad and shove off early.

"I've got math homework," I say. "See ya."

Cam's the only one to say goodbye. Things are really bad when math is more appealing than hanging with your friends. If they're still my friends.

I can't believe the attitude, but I'm going to stop thinking about it. They'll come around—I know they will. And I might as well do math while I can, because I won't have much time for it once rehearsals start. At the door, I take a look back over my shoulder, then wish I hadn't. My whole table is quiet, watching me leave. And I hear Mavis say, just loud enough to reach my ears, "This is all we need. As if his head isn't big enough!"

* * *

Class that afternoon is devoted to preparing for the dance exams, which is incredibly boring. I hate dance exams. Doing the moves in front of a panel of grumpy old dancers seems so fake, but it's a requirement, and Mr. Colson expects us to take it seriously. Odette shines at this kind of work. I bet if she were a pianist, she'd love doing scales all day long. She's that sort of girl. Usually Charis and I make funny faces at each other in the mirror to make the time go by, but today she won't let me catch her eye.

After class I grab Charis's arm. "Hey, you missed my best face!" I leer at her.

"You're ridiculous," she says with disdain. "Do you honestly think the company's going to appreciate that sort of nonsense?"

"Not you too! Come on, Charis. I thought we were friends."

She whirls around, looking so fierce that I drop her arm and put my hands up in surrender. "Whoa! Calm down!"

"Friends? You're such an idiot. We've never been friends, not ever. Don't you see?"

"No, I don't see." I really am confused. "Pizza? Pranks? A couple of laughs so we don't think about how much our bodies hurt? Eating meals together, sharing class? That's not friends?"

"No. That's not friends," Charis says, slumping a little. "That's pals. And it's okay to be pals, for a while anyway, but we can never be friends. None of us can."

"That's stupid."

"Think about it. We all want to dance. There are twenty of us in our year alone. How many places open up in the company each year? Not twenty, that's for sure. This isn't a team situation—it's a competition. A competition for our futures, and we only get one chance." Charis puts her back to the wall and slides dejectedly down on her heels. "Maybe you don't get it because you're a guy. Cam doesn't want to be in the company, and there's probably room for both you and Jeremy, because you two are the best of the senior boys. But us girls? There are dozens of us for every single spot. How do you think I'm going to feel when Sybille and Johanna and I are all trying to get the last place in the company? If I get the place, they'll hate me. If one of them gets it, I'll hate them. We can't be friends, Rob. It will hurt too much in the end."

I slide down to the floor beside her. Why do girls make everything so complicated? "I still don't get it. You and I don't have to compete, so can't we be friends at least?"

Charis shakes her head sadly. "Girls can play Puck too, you know. I mean, Puck's a fairy, for heaven's sake! Who knows if fairies even have genders? If I'd been given this chance, I'd have a real leg up for a company spot. You don't need this break, but I do. I'm sorry, Rob, but I wish it was me instead of you. They probably only gave it to you because they wanted Rick in the role, and it was easier to have a male understudy."

"Gee, thanks, Charis," I reply sarcastically. "Appreciate the support."

"It's the truth, Rob. Face it. Right place, right time. You got lucky, that's all."

I'm trying to process this as Sybille and Johanna spot us hunkered down on the floor. "So this is where you got to!" they say, each taking an arm and pulling Charis up. They ignore me completely. "Come on, we're going to the gym."

As Charis heads off toward the gym, arms linked with Sybille and Johanna, she turns back to me. "I've got to go with my *pals*."

I watch them go. Maybe she's right. But girls' logic makes me so confused that I really don't know what to think.

*   *   *

Since everybody's going to the gym, I decide to skip it. Instead, I head to the park around the corner from the school. It used to be where the smokers hung out, but hardly anybody smokes anymore, which means there'll be no dancers but me. I pull out my cell phone.

"Hey, Mom," I say. "How're you doing?"

"Fine, dear. Where are the boys?"

Normally, Jeremy, Cam and I video chat with my mom together. She's kind of adopted both of them—Cam even calls her Mom—but I don't want them to bring her down like they have me.

"Oh, they're around. I've got some news."

"Yes?"

"You won't believe it. I'm going to understudy Puck for the company's next performance!"

Mom squeals, and I can hear her yelling for my dad and my brothers. "You've got to hear this!" she's shouting. "Robin, I'm putting you on speakerphone! Hurry up, men! Okay, Robin, they're here. Tell us everything."

This is what I wanted, what I needed. I tell them about Noah, the prank ("Robin, you didn't!"), the meeting with Bellamy Acton ("Mom, he said pranking made me perfect for the role!"), the contract, the rehearsal schedule and Rick Mathews, the dancer I'm shadowing.

"You mean, you're like a bench player?" asks one of my brothers.

"Yeah, sort of," I reply. "I'll only dance if he gets hurt or can't go on for some reason. But it means I train with the company, and they get to know me. It's huge."

"What about Jeremy and Cam?" asks Mom. "Are they understudies as well?"

"No, only me. I guess they didn't need any other students."

"Oh! They must be so excited for you!" says Mom proudly.

Yeah right. Sure they are. Why do you think I'm out here by myself?

"Do you need me to help with your costume?" Mom asks. "I kind of miss the old days when I got to sew your costumes."

Inwardly I groan. She has got to be kidding. "Mom, this is the company. The *company*, get it? They have a whole team of designers and seamstresses to do the costumes."

"Yes, but I've seen their costumes. Ridiculous, some of them. And others are so very plain. You know I could do better."

I have to smile. Mom is great. Honestly, she'd have me in sequins, given half a chance. She'd have my brothers' whole football team in sequins if she thought she could get away with it.

She's a madwoman when she has a needle in her hand. I can almost hear my brothers snickering in the background—I know they're thinking the same thing.

"You know it only takes two hours to drive in to the city. We'll be buying tickets, of course, so let me know when they go on sale."

"Mom, that's great, but remember, I'm not dancing. I'm just the understudy. Okay?"

"Robin, for heaven's sake, I know what an understudy is. But it's a perfect opportunity to get some culture into these three oafs you left me with. And you never know—maybe you *will* dance."

"Mom!" shouts one of my brothers. "Don't say that! It's bad luck!"

"Yeah, and offense can't afford any more bad luck, can it, bro?"

I hear my brothers start going at it in the background. "What's that about?" I ask.

Dad answers. "There's been a string of injuries on the football team. So many that even the coach is getting superstitious about it. It's a bad blow, but I have to say that the whole woo-woo sentiment has been pretty amusing for the rest of us."

For the first time ever, I wish I was home and not at Premier. Making fun of my brothers, laughing together, cheering at their games, rolling our eyes at Mom's weird notions while we love her to bits...I miss it. So we talk about football and Mom's lasagna and Aunt Sally's gallbladder and the neighbor's dog and a million other inconsequential things until my cell dies. And, with it, my good mood.

Five

I try not to be nervous about warming up with the company. As the only student understudy, I'm going to be completely on my own. But no worries. I'm going to prove them all wrong. I deserve this chance, and I'm not going to fool around and blow it. So I'm in the company studio early, in full uniform, completely warmed up. I am ready.

The company dancers start to wander into the studio in twos and threes, and my heart sinks. Of course company dancers don't wear the school uniform. Jeremy could have—should have—told me that. I look ridiculous in my white T-shirt, black tights and mid-calf white socks. They don't even wear leather ballet slippers, only canvas. Everything they wear is ripped and torn, and they have more layers on than an onion has skin. Most of the girls have topped their wooly layers with garbage-bag pants and shawls to keep the heat in. As if Mr. Colson would ever allow the girls in my class to dress like that! The guys are wearing torn sweats—at least I own some of those. I am absolutely not wearing uniform tomorrow.

Some of the dancers smile at me, and a couple even come over to say congratulations. They know better than anybody how it feels to get your first big break. It's so totally cool. I stay at the barre but keep an eye on the other warm-ups. One of the guys is using a Nalgene water bottle to roll out his calves, and a girl is using pink rubber balls to roll out her feet. I can't wait to tell Charis—she'll like that. Another girl is dancing with toe spacers, and man, that's got to hurt. But I guess it helps when you're wearing pointe shoes. If guys have to do double tours, it's fair that girls have to wear pointe shoes.

When Mr. Acton comes in, I'm relieved. This is a long warm-up, and even with all the weird stuff going on around me, I'm running out of ideas. It would probably look really lame if I started to copy what they're doing.

Class is no different than it is in the school: same exercises, same music. Ballet is all about doing things the same way they have always been done, so I'm good here. My first correction makes my heart lurch, but Mr. Acton corrects other dancers too, so it's not only me. The most unbelievable thing is that the dancers wander away from the barre from time to time and do their own thing—like rolling out their hips—then wander back, and Mr. Acton doesn't even seem to mind. Then the music stops.

All the dancers collapse, or, I should say, sink gracefully to the floor. They are *so* good. Mr. Acton brings up a chair and starts to talk about the story-line of the ballet. I try to keep all the characters straight. There's the Duke of Athens, who is getting married. There are two guys and two girls; one couple is eloping, and the other is chasing them. Oberon and Titania are the King and Queen of the Fairies, but they're in the middle of a huge fight. Finally, there's a troupe of actors doing a play within the play, making fun of everything that's going down. All these people are in the forest, either going to or running away from the Duke's wedding. Then there's Puck. Oberon asks him to make a love potion, but Puck messes it up and gets all the wrong people in love with each other. It takes the rest of the dance to straighten things out.

Sounds perfect for me.

Mr. Acton talks about his vision for the piece and the direction he wants to go with it. Then he gives a speech about how each actor needs to bring "vitality, honesty and freshness" to their role. He gives everybody a copy of the play to read after class, then asks the dancers to experiment with different types of movement that might suit their character. They start to move around the room, and their eyes get kind of unfocused. This is so weird. Some people are playing around with jerky hops, others are waving their arms around in silly romantic port de bras, and some are simply moving about. All the dancers are totally getting into character. And Rick is amazing as Puck. He makes all these quick little motions with his hands, and he jumps up and down, and he hides. He's even started poking the other dancers, just like Puck does. He really is a sprite. Watching these dancers create something from nothing is amazing.

But it's also terrifying. I don't know what to do. I'm used to learning steps, then adding interpretation at the end. In company class, everything is backward, and I feel like an idiot, standing around watching. All of a sudden, Puck pokes me from behind. I swing around, kind of mad because I was startled, and Puck is hiding behind one of the other dancers, waggling his eyebrows at me. Without thinking, I go for him. He dashes around to the other side of the barre. We do this kind of mirror thing, poking at each other from opposite sides of the barre, and then he dashes away again. I leap after him, only to skid to an abrupt stop. Puck's hiding behind Mr. Acton, who's standing there staring at me, arms crossed. Game over.

But then he smiles, and Rick comes out from behind him. "Not bad, kid," says Rick as he walks away.

All I can do is stare after him. *Wow.*

I bet we could do this with our year-end performance. Odette always knows everything, so she can lead the discussion about vision and direction and everything, and then we can all try getting into character for our parts. And I can't wait to tell my friends about the warm-up. There's stuff we could copy. This is going to be great.

Six

'm late and have to run to catch the school bus the next morning, plunking down in the empty seat in front of Cam and Jeremy just before the bus lumbers away from the curb. That's what happens when you stay up half the night reading a play.

"You missed breakfast," says Cam. "Here." He hands me a greasy fried-egg sandwich, still warm.

"Thanks," I say, licking the ketchup that's already running down my hand. "I think."

"Where were you?"

"Slept in," I mumble, up to my elbows in drippy sandwich. "Up late."

"Got your English essay?" asks Jeremy.

"Darn! I forgot."

Odette's sitting in the seat across from me, alone and studying, as usual. Without taking her eyes from her book, she says, "So, big stars don't have to do homework anymore?" Then she looks up and makes a face at my sloppy sandwich. "You are *so* disgusting!"

I ignore her and lick my fingers. "Thanks, Cam. Listen, company rehearsal is amazing. It's so different from ours. Everybody's allowed to do their own warm-ups, and there's no uniform. And it's all about interpretation, not the steps. We haven't even learned any of the choreography yet, but everybody's already getting into character."

"You're in the big leagues now, buddy," Cam says, grinning. "Not like us poor suckers! Do you think Mrs. Montgomery will give you detention?"

"No way she'll ever let one of the dreaded ballet students have an extension," replies Jeremy curtly. "You're toast."

I shrug my shoulders and turn around in my seat. Who cares about an English essay? Or Mrs. Montgomery's crazy hatred of the half-day ballet students who mess up her approach to teaching? We're ballet dancers, not novelists. I turn around again to tell them more about the rehearsal, but they both have their noses buried in books. It's not like we have a lot of time to do homework, I get that, but how can they not be interested? I turn around once more, sigh and pull out my science textbook.

I can't actually do detention because I have rehearsal, so Mrs. Montgomery gleefully assigns me an extra essay on top of the one that's already not done. As if that's going to work. I get most of my math done on the bus ride back to the ballet school. First up this afternoon is pas de deux class. Dancing a duet is new to us, and it involves working on lifts with the girls, which will be cool. After that is supper, then company rehearsal. I can't wait.

*   *   *

Everybody stares when I walk into class. I mean, I knew they would, since I'm wearing my torn sweats over my uniform.

"The company takes warming up really seriously," I explain. "I think Mr. Colson should let us layer up a little more."

"*You* think?" Odette sneers. "One rehearsal and you're an expert now?"

"Well, it works! I feel looser when I'm warmer. We're here to learn new things, aren't we?"

"Yeah," she shoots back, "but I trust my teachers to know what's best for me, not you. You're a real dork, you know that, Robin?"

That's the cue for Cam and Jeremy to get my back. Cam gives me a sheepish half smile but says nothing. Jeremy studiously concentrates on his warm-up. Odette raises her eyebrows and smirks at me, then gets to her warm-up as well. *Fine.*

Mr. Colson comes in then and finishes off our warm-up with some group exercises. Then he pairs us up for the pas de deux.

"Ladies, you'll have to take turns with the men," says Mr. Colson. "Use the barre to practice the positions until your turn."

Cam lets out this big sigh, then says just loudly enough for everybody to hear, "Another class where the boys have to work harder than the girls." He rolls his eyes dramatically. "And yet the audience will never look past the tutu to see the crane that does the heavy lifting."

Odette spins around with a glare, prepared to defend the girls, but we're already laughing. Even Mr. Colson is hiding a smile. It's my chance to get back at her.

"Mr. Colson, I've been watching weight lifters on TV. Do we lift the girls like that? You know, with a snatch and jerk? Can we make faces and grunt, then drop them when they get too heavy?" Even Jeremy can't help busting a gut at that one.

"Enough nonsense!" says Mr. Colson firmly. He starts to show us the lifting positions, and Jer whispers, "Weight lifters have it so easy compared to us!"

I grin. It feels like old times, horsing around in class. But the moment doesn't last.

"Odette, you start with Jeremy," orders Mr. Colson. "Mavis, you're with Cam, and Johanna, you go with Robin." As Mr. Colson continues matching girls with boys, Johanna makes her way over toward me. But talk about attitude! She's rolling her eyes and grimacing as if partnering with me is the worst thing that could ever happen to her. *Gee, thanks, Johanna.*

I love you too. I feel like dropping her accidentally-on-purpose, but I'm better than that.

Mr. Colson goes over correct hand position for the gazillionth time. "Cup your hands, men, no splayed fingers. If you lift with your finger-tips, your partner will have five little bruises on each side of her waist tomorrow, and you do not want that to happen! Men, it is simply *not* worth the aggravation!"

It isn't easy to get a grip with a cupped hand, so we're only lifting the girls four inches or so off the floor. But Cam and Jer and I have been hitting the gym—well, except for yesterday—and I feel strong. Johanna and I try a little higher, a little higher, and I'm almost to the point where I can lift her right over my head, but Mr. Colson says no, not yet. But it's coming, I know it. By the end of the afternoon, lifting with cupped hands feels almost normal.

Between classes, I grab Charis's arm. "Wait up! I wanted to tell you—the company dancers use these little pink balls to roll out their feet. And they dance with toe spacers—Charis, you should really watch the company warm-up. It's so cool, and I know you'd learn a lot."

Charis raises her eyebrows. "Thanks for the tip. And here I thought I'd learned everything already."

"I was only trying to help. Just because I'm the one that got the part doesn't mean we can't all get something out of it."

"Yeah, well, you don't need to rub it in."

Rolling my eyes, I go over to the corner and slump down on the floor beside Cam and Jer. I brought my water bottle today, and I start rolling out my calves with it. They stare. "This is how the company guys do it," I explain.

"Ah," says Cam. "Probably not a technique us poor students will be able to master then."

"Give me a break!" I explode. "I am not trying to rub it in! Can I help it if I'm learning new things? What, you want me to pretend I'm not part of the company?"

"Yeah, that might be an idea," says Jeremy. They both get up and walk to the barre together.

I don't believe it. All of a sudden my friends think I'm too good for them? Well, stuff them. I'm part of the company, at least for now, and if they don't like it, tough.

Seven

I've never been so happy to be ignored.

They go so fast. The company, I mean. Mr. Acton shows the choreography once—*once*—and we're expected to have the steps memorized. And sometimes he doesn't even show us—he just lists all the steps in order, and we have to imagine them in our heads. Then perform them. Instantly. Are they all geniuses or something? I can't process that fast. I bet everybody else will have the choreography for the entire production learned in a week, and I'll still be marking the first act. I feel like such a moron.

"Oops, sorry!"

"Wrong way, kid."

I want to die.

"No, no, no!" shouts Mr. Acton. Everybody stops. "This is all wrong!"

Luckily, he's not looking at me in particular. I ease backward into a corner, behind the other understudies. The back row is ours and ours alone, and I am *so* glad. The principals are pacing at the front of the room.

"This isn't Baby Ballet, people! I need you to eat space. You must gobble up the stage! Move, move, move! Nothing small. Go deep, move it across the floor like you've never done before! And in the fondu—both legs straighten at the same time. You *know* that! We need to go back to the basics." Mr. Acton sighs. "Chassé, coupé, pas de bourrée, jeté. *Now!*" We all line up in the corner. I am so relieved. These steps I can do. It's just like class.

Back and forth, back and forth. Leaping, jumping, turning. The studio reeks of sweat and we're all panting, but Mr. Acton keeps shouting, "Again! Again!" Finally, we get a take-ten. Everybody collapses, but I'm feeling okay. I'm good at cross floor, and I can keep up. But, of course, the minute I start feeling halfway like a company member, Mr. Acton takes it all away.

"Rick, Robin," he says. "Let's go over the scene where Oberon gives the flower to Puck."

As I mark the steps, trying to follow Rick's every amazing move, there's a flicker at the window. I think I see Jeremy. *Please don't let him be watching this.*

*   *   *

Mr. Acton stops me after rehearsal. "How are you feeling?" he asks.

"Great!" I lie enthusiastically. "It's fantastic to watch the company work. I'm learning so much, Mr. Acton."

He looks at me thoughtfully. "But are you learning fast enough, Robin?" he asks gently. "This isn't simply another class. You have to take ownership of your role, even if you're only the understudy. You have to be just as ready as Rick to perform. Are you?"

I don't say anything. It's pretty obvious that I'm not.

"What's your biggest struggle?"

"The choreography," I mumble. "The company dancers pick it up so fast."

"That can be fixed, if you're willing to put in extra time," replies Mr. Acton. "I have a video of the choreography. You can borrow it, if you want, and learn the steps on your own time. It's much harder that way, but I don't have time to walk you through it. You need to have the steps down before you can become the character, and you have a long way to go."

No one, *no one*, has ever had to say stuff like that to me before. I've always been the best. Always. This sucks. We walk in silence to his office to get the disc, because there's really nothing more to say.

*   *   *

Rehearsal isn't over until eight, and I have an English essay—no, make that *two* English essays—to write for tomorrow. Well, forget that. Mrs. Montgomery can yell all she wants. Maybe I'll skip and get in some extra rehearsal time. But somehow, I don't feel like I can wait until tomorrow. I shower because I'm so gross, then head back to the dark, empty studio, the one that has the DVD player. I'll work all night if I have to.

Mr. Acton is right. It's hard to learn chore-ography from video. Thank goodness for remote control. I may totally wear out the Stop button. Still, without everybody watching me, I can actu-ally think. I take it step by step, cutting the work into tiny pieces. But there are so many pieces! And the Puck on the video is distracting. He's really good, and his footwork is clean, but his Puck is so different from Rick's. Which one is right?

Maybe it would be easier to turn the TV toward the mirror and watch the reflection. At least then I won't be learning the steps backward. *Good one, brainiac—the remote won't work that way.* But I try it anyway. This is what despera-tion looks like, I guess.

It's eerie to work all alone in the middle of the night. I'm so used to having Cam and Jeremy right beside me that I don't even jump when I hear their voices. But they're not talking to me. They're outside. I go over to the window, and by the light of the moon, I see them. It's Cam, Jer, Johanna, Charis and Sybille. My gang. They're laughing, then covering their mouths with their hands to deaden the sound. Half-crouching, they're running across the quad toward the kitchen.

Midnight raid! All right! I need a break. I shut down the DVD player, lock the studio and return the key. No point in changing, because it's not like we don't breathe each other's sweat all day, every day anyway.

By the time I get to the kitchen, they're into the ice cream. "Hey," I say.

There's silence. Finally Cam says, "Hey yourself."

"So...midnight raid."

"Yeah, we were in the mood," says Charis. "Too bad you can't join us. We know you're busy, you know, with the company and all."

"Ah, yeah," I reply. "I was rehearsing when I heard you guys laughing. You know Miss Amelia's room is beside the kitchen. You gotta keep it quiet when you cross the quad. Did I not teach you anything?" I try to make it into a joke, but nobody's laughing.

"Thanks for the tip," says Charis sarcastically. "We would never have thought of that without your help."

No, you wouldn't have! I shout to myself. *I* was the one who started the midnight raids. *I* was the one who found out where the kitchen key is hidden. *I* was the one who picked the route so we'd never get caught. It's *my* raid!

"Well, I guess I have more work to do," I say. "Enjoy your ice cream."

"Oh, we will," replies Charis. She's so smug.

"Gee, Charis, you sound just like Odette," I say, and I'm glad when I see the hurt on her face.

Eight

Breakfast is a quiet affair. Everybody's so busy not talking to me that they're not talking to each other either. Halfway through my poached eggs, these two little girls from the junior school come up to my table, giggling.

"Are you the guy dancing Puck?" they ask. "Can we have your autograph?"

Hey, my first autograph! "Sure," I say and reach for the paper and pen they push toward me.

"You know he's only the understudy, don't you?" Charis says.

The girls giggle in reply and run off.

"Cute," says Johanna. "Rob's got his own little fan club. Too bad they're only nine!"

Everybody at the table laughs.

Fine. Who needs breakfast anyway? I push off from the table and go back to my dorm for my English papers. After being uninvited to the raid, I couldn't sleep. So I wrote. The essays are bad but done. Maybe somebody will be happy with me today.

The dorm's empty as I grab my stuff and stuff it into my backpack. I put the play in too. Looks like I'll have more time to study it between classes, because I'll probably be uninvited to the cafeteria too. On the way to the bus, I decide to check the company bulletin board in case I missed anything, and as I turn down the hall that leads to the office, I hear arguing. Just in time, I pull back around the corner. It sounds like Jeremy's mom.

"That boy is your stiffest competition for the company. How could you have let him get this part? Why not you? Aren't you working hard enough? Are you having trouble? You have to *tell* me if you need help, Jeremy!"

"Mom, stop it!" That voice is Jeremy's. "Of course I'm working. And I'm not having trouble with anything! None of us knew that Noah was going to wreck his tendon, so we could hardly plan for this. Rob got picked. Not me. It's not like I could do anything about it."

"Yes, Jeremy, you certainly could have done something about it. If you really wanted to be a principal, you would *always* be ready for opportunity. Clearly, you're not. Are we wasting our time with you? Is ballet not what you want?"

"I don't know, Mom," says Jeremy rudely. "It looks like you want it enough for both of us."

I can hear Jeremy's mom gasp. I kind of feel like gasping too, because that was such a non-Jeremy thing to say.

Then I hear her answer. "I'm sorry," she says. "I know you're working hard. But try to be ready the next time. Which might be soon, by the way. I hear your friend is having a hard time keeping up with the company. I doubt he'll get another chance."

Great. Just great.

*   *   *

The closer we get to performance day, the more rehearsals there are. I don't go to my regular classes anymore, which is a relief. I've got enough to worry about, and I don't need any more grief. I skip lunch and book the rehearsal studio with the DVD player to go over the steps again. I think I have them—most of them anyway. Part of me says it doesn't matter. As the understudy, I'm here to learn, not perform. But the other part of me knows that's lame. I have to do well, or Jeremy's mom will be right. I'll never get picked again.

The company dancers drag in to evening rehearsal. I've heard the principals talking to some of the newer dancers, and they say this is the slog time. It happens about two weeks before opening and lasts a week, long enough for everybody to start panicking that the production will be a flop. And even though I'm only an understudy, I'm starting to panic a little bit myself. Nobody has any energy, and even the really good dancers are walking through their choreography instead of dancing it. Cripes, if this was class, Mr. Colson would be all over us, but Mr. Acton lets everybody do their own thing. I guess he's seen the slump before.

"Are you sure this is normal?" I ask Rick as we practice the steps in Puck's final solo.

"Don't worry," Rick reassures me. "It happens every production."

We have time to go through the steps by ourselves two more times before Mr. Acton calls for the solo. Rick takes his place in the center of the studio to wait for the music, and I fade into the back corner where no one can see me. This solo is the one I absolutely hate, because it ends in the double tour. Why, why do guys have to do this? But it's easy for Rick; he can fly through the air with no problem at all. I mimic the steps while he dances, and the other understudies give me a wide berth. Unfortunately, they've seen my double tour before. *Concentrate!* Feet in fifth position, plié, then rotate. Twice. Weight even on both sides. Breathe.

I'm concentrating so hard that I barely hear the other dancers gasp. *I did it! I did it!* I want to shout it out to the world. It was my best double tour ever, and they all saw it! But when I refocus, it's pretty clear that those gasps were not for me. All eyes are on Rick. It takes a minute for me to figure out what's going on. Everybody's watching Rick, all right, but that's because he's lying in a heap on the floor.

Mr. Acton's kneeling beside him, and Rick is absolutely white.

"Is it broken?" he moans. "Tell me it isn't broken!"

Mr. Acton has Rick's foot in his hand. I can't really see through all the people, but I sure can hear when Mr. Acton presses the wrong spot. Rick shrieks and practically passes out.

"It's broken," says Mr. Acton quietly.

There are gasps and groans from the company dancers. Then every head turns to look at me.

Nine

"**N**o!"

I'm sitting straight up, staring at the wall, and I feel sick to my stomach. Sweat is pouring off me, and my heart is pounding. Man, what a horrible dream.

I take deep breaths and try to untangle the covers. My bed looks like I had a major fight with a wildcat or something. It isn't until I'm awake enough to change my sweaty T-shirt that the sick feeling rolls over me again. Rick really did break his ankle, and I really do have to dance. It was no dream.

The looks the company dancers gave me when it hit them that I was their guy? I'll never forget their faces. Disbelief, anger, horror—even pity. Yeah, pity. This was supposed to be my big break, but everybody knows I can't cut it. They don't want me in the part. Heck, I don't want me in the part. Because I can't do it.

Rick was so amazing. There's no way I can be as good. I barely know the steps, I've never practiced the lifts for real, nobody wants to work with me, and oh yeah, I've only landed a double tour once in my whole life. Don't forget that.

I crawl back into bed with a clean shirt and curl up under the covers. My options are limited. If I go on, it will be the end of my career as a dancer, not to mention making sure that the whole production is a flop and the company loses all kinds of money and rep because I'm so lousy. If I don't go on, it will be the end of my career as a dancer, not to mention making sure that the whole production is a flop and the company loses all kinds of money and rep because they haven't got anybody else to dance the part. Hmm, do I or don't I? My life sucks.

I have to say, though, that deep down there's a little part of me that's excited. I'm talking really deep. But this is the dream, isn't it? An accidental chance that changes your life? The thing is, in the fairy tale the guy with the chance is a star.

I really, really want to be that guy. But there's no point in kidding myself. I'm not.

* * *

At breakfast, it's clear that the word is out. My so-called friends are in shock.

"What happened?" Jeremy asks. Another accident in the company has clearly put him over the edge. He's practically hyperventilating.

"I don't know." I shrug my shoulders. "It was on the double tour, I think. I landed mine, but Rick ended up on the floor. How weird is that?"

"Yeah, and it's always all about you, isn't it?" Odette says with disgust. "We're all so glad that you, at least, landed *yours*."

"Come on, Odette, you know I didn't mean it that way."

"Really? When now you get to be the star of the show? Of course you didn't mean it that way," she scoffs as she picks up her tray to go.

Charis picks up her tray as well. "Honestly, Rob," she says, "nobody ever thought you were going to have to dance. What's Mr. Acton going to do?"

"A little support from my friends would be nice," I say sarcastically. I can't let her know I'm wondering the same thing. Right now, I'd give my big break to anybody stupid enough to take it.

The other girls start loading dirty plates onto trays, all except Sybille. She doesn't move from her seat across the table.

"Good work," she says angrily.

"What are you talking about?"

"Rick. He's ten times the dancer you are. You must have really wanted the part."

I don't believe this. "What? You think I *arranged* for him to break his ankle? Put out a hit or something? Are you absolutely out of your mind?"

"Well, it's pretty convenient, isn't it? Now you get to be the big star and save the show. Just like in the movies. You're no better than any of us, Robin Goodman, so I know there's more to this story."

"Yeah, the rest of the story is that you're not ready to give up this week's heartthrob, but you can't let yourself be in love with somebody on the injured list. You're whacked out, Sybille."

I must have said it louder than I intended, because in an instant Jeremy is up from his chair.

"She is not!"

"Oh, come on. She thinks I somehow broke Rick's ankle so I could get the part. As if. That's flat-out crazy."

Now it's Charis jumping to her defense. "Why are you picking on Sybille?"

Unbelievable. "I'm *not* picking on her. She's picking on *me*. What is this, gang-up-on-Rob day? Why don't you just leave me alone?"

So they do. They all head out of the cafeteria, until the only other person left from my class is Odette, who, like me, is sitting alone at a table. Our eyes meet, but for once she doesn't say a word.

*   *   *

After breakfast there's a big meeting. The whole company is milling about in the big rehearsal studio, looking not so much angry as defeated. Rick's ankle has guaranteed that the production will be a flop, since I'm going to make them look bad no matter how hard they work. Mr. Acton, Mr. Colson and Miss Amelia are at the front, and even Rick is here, sitting in a wheelchair, his cast covered in autographs. He still looks pretty white.

He wheels himself over and parks himself beside me, which makes me feel a little better.

"You're going to be okay, kid," he says quietly. "We'll make sure of it."

I sure hope he's right, but I don't know where he thinks this miracle is going to come from. Because that's what it is going to take. The way I see it, Noah was strike one, Rick was strike two, and I'm going to be strike three for the Premier Dance Company.

The dancer playing Titania speaks up first. "No offense, Robin, because you've worked super hard, but we all know you're not ready for this. Bellamy, what if we were to rearrange the parts so that Francis Flute plays Peter Quince, Peter Quince plays Demetrius, Demetrius plays Bottom, and Bottom plays Puck? Then Robin could play Francis Flute, which isn't such a big part. He could handle it."

Mr. Acton sighs. "We're less than two weeks from opening. That would mean that every major male role would be weak, with all of you scrambling to learn new choreography. Better that we have only one weak dancer and all of us help him to give his best."

Titania sighs. "This is a disaster," she says under her breath.

I totally agree with her. I'm not even upset about being called weak anymore.

"Maybe we could keep most of the male roles intact but put one of us from the chorus in for Puck. We can all learn the part fast enough."

Okay, so this suggestion makes me bristle. It's coming from David, one of the weakest of the company dancers. He's no better a dancer than I am, even if he can learn choreography faster. He's only trying to take advantage.

"Hey, I have an idea!" someone else says. "Why don't we let Rick play the role from a wheelchair? That would be a neat twist!" Everybody laughs but me. My dancing is so bad that even a guy in a wheelchair is better? I want to die.

Mr. Acton calms everybody down, then looks at me. It's my turn to talk, and I've rehearsed in my head what I'm going to say. I know I can't go on. It's not because I'm scared. If it were just me, I'd go out there, even if I flopped. But it's not just me, it's the company. And I'm going to ruin the production for everybody.

I stand up. My mouth feels dry, and it's hard to swallow. I know I'll never get another chance like this, but I have to do what's right. I take a deep breath, open my mouth, and all the wrong words fall out.

"I know I'm not nearly as good as all of you, and I'm scared to death I'll wreck the whole production. But if you'll help me, I'll work day and night to get it right."

Silence first, and then the whole room erupts in cheers. Rick is grinning crazily, Mr. Acton is smiling, and the others (except maybe David) look like, well, like maybe it will be okay.

What have I done?

* * *

Rick, Mr. Acton and I go to one of the rehearsal rooms by ourselves while Miss Amelia takes over rehearsing the rest of the company.

"Robin, let's start with the flower scene. We need to go over all of your choreography to see what parts you've got down, what parts need work and what parts, if any, we need to remove or change."

Read: parts you're so bad at that we have to take them out.

At first it's hard to dance when I can't hide in the back row like a good little understudy. Mr. Acton's eyes are like solar flares, way fiercer than Odette's puny glares. When I miss a step, Rick yells it out from his wheelchair, and that's okay, because it's only us in the studio. After a bit, having two amazing teachers all to myself starts to feel good. Everything's going great until he starts calling in other dancers to work with me.

First it's Bottom. Bottom's character is supposed to be really funny. He has to pretend that he's the best at everything but then make all sorts of ridiculous mistakes to make the audience laugh. Puck's character uses magic to turn Bottom's head into a donkey's head, making him look even more ridiculous. The scene is really comical, and when Rick and the dancer playing Bottom do the scene, it's hilarious. But I'm terrified.

Mr. Acton motions for the music to start, and Bottom starts strutting around the studio. I can't stop laughing. Everything he does is funny, and I'm in awe. I tiptoe around him, staying out of the limelight, waiting for my cue to sneak up behind him. Then I lift the fake donkey's head to slip it over Bottom's real head. Unfortunately, I don't lift it high enough and practically knock the poor guy out with the prop.

"No!" shouts Mr. Acton. "Do it again!" Bottom gives me back the donkey's head and I try to remember how Rick did it, but he's getting mixed up in my head with the Puck on the DVD. I have no idea what I'm doing.

After a break, Mr. Acton calls in Peaseblossom, one of the fairies, to rehearse with me. She looks like a thundercloud.

"Can he do it, Bellamy? I mean, really do it?" she asks, as if I'm not there. "I hate dancing with amateurs."

"Give the boy a chance," replies Mr. Acton. "You had a first time too, remember."

"Yes, but I wasn't as green as this," Peaseblossom retorts.

"Nor were you sixteen years old," says Mr. Acton sharply. "Take your place. Now."

Puck doesn't really have any pas de deux sections, thank goodness, but there are a couple of small lifts. I'm trying to remember what Mr. Colson said about hand placement, weight and balance, but the music isn't giving me time, so in the end I just grab Peaseblossom and heft her up. It's only a waist-high lift, not a biggie, and I think I'm pretty smooth, but all of a sudden Peaseblossom yelps.

"Let go of me!"

I practically drop her.

"You oaf! Bellamy, this isn't going to work! Look what he's done to me!" Peaseblossom pulls her top out of her tights, baring her waist. "Ten perfect bruises—on the very first lift! That's a newbie mistake. Bellamy, he's not ready!"

Well, thanks for all the support, I feel like saying. *No way you've got ten bruises two seconds after I let go.* But I did forget to cup my hands. I know I didn't do it right, but honestly, I've only had two classes on lifts! Give me a break.

By the end of the day I'm so tired I can hardly see straight, but Mr. Acton decides to let me go back into the regular rehearsal for some general practice. And I'm glad. I don't want to worry about the choreography or the character or who's going to be my next guinea pig. I just want to dance.

Finally, Mr. Acton says, "That will be enough for today, everyone. Thank you very much."

As we pack up our stuff, I hear Peaseblossom and Titania talking quietly. "Yeah, but he's a great mover," says Titania.

I know what that means. You say somebody's a great mover when they have natural talent, but it's not trained. It's an insult made to sound like praise. Trouble is, being a natural isn't enough anymore.

After showering, I grab a sandwich from the cafeteria and take it into the rehearsal room with the DVD player. Not allowed, but I couldn't care less. As I eat, I watch the DVD over and over. I promised them I would work all day and all night, and I will.

Ten

Rick's exhausted and Mr. Acton's frustrated. They say I'm trying too hard, but I don't understand what they mean. How can you try too hard? The one thing I know for sure is that I hate dance. And this dance school. I'm seriously wishing I could wreck my ankle too.

Opening night is less than a week away. Maybe I could starve myself and drop from exhaustion. The fish sticks and mashed potatoes on my dinner tray look disgusting, but Mr. Acton says I have to eat, that I'm losing weight. I haven't had time to go to the gym—I haven't had time to do *anything*—but he says I have to make time to eat. But I can't—it's too gross. I push my tray away, grab my cell phone and head for the park.

"Hey, Mom," I say.

"What's wrong?"

How is it that moms always know? "Just tired."

"I haven't heard from you in ages, and that's a sure sign you're pushing yourself. You'll be no good onstage if you're exhausted, Robin."

Yeah, but exhaustion isn't what I'm worried about.

"After you phoned to say you were actually dancing, I called everybody in the family! We've all got tickets now. Aunt Sally, Uncle Harry, your cousins, Melissa—remember your old baby-sitter?—my friend Martha, her husband..."

Mom goes on and on. How do I break in and tell her I'm quitting? That I'm no good, that I can't cut it as a dancer? That everybody hates me?

"Mom, hang on a minute, there's something..."

"And we've all decided to book rooms at that swanky hotel near the theater, I can't remember the name offhand. It's expensive, but it's not every day your boy has his debut, is it?"

"Mom, wait..."

"Do you know what your costume looks like? I've checked online, and you sure see a lot of different costumes for Puck. Are they going for green? You've always looked good in green."

I can't do it.

"Yes, I have my costume. I think you'll be surprised, Mom. In fact, I know you will."

"Hmmm. That sounds ominous. Anyway, listen to me go on. What were you calling about?"

"Nothing, Mom. Just wanted to hear your voice."

"Isn't that sweet? I'm sending a hug your way, Robin. Now get to bed. You need to sleep. Pleasant dreams, and we'll see you soon."

Sleep. Sure. I head back to the boys' change room. I should go to the company change room, but I don't think I can stand anybody's comments tonight, and the boys' change room should be empty.

I pull on my warm-ups, but I don't know if I can face more practice tonight. I'm done. I can't even get up from the bench. Everything aches, mostly my heart. Dance is over for me.

All of a sudden the door opens and Jeremy and Cam burst in, talking a mile a minute. *Great.* They stop short when they see me.

"Why aren't you in the company dressing room?" asks Jeremy.

"I didn't feel like going there."

"What, the company doesn't think you're such a hotshot now that you actually have to perform?" Jeremy says snidely.

"Maybe I'm sick of them."

Cam looks a little shocked.

"You're an idiot," retorts Jeremy. "You're the one who gets the big chance, and now you're sick of it? I don't think hotshots are allowed to be sick of it. *I never pegged you as the jealous type.* Remember that? *This is how the company guys do it.* Sweet. You were so smart, and now you've decided to give up because you're *sick of them*? Dancers don't give up—ever."

"Proves I'm not a dancer, doesn't it?" I shoot back.

"Hey, guys," says Cam. "Chill."

There is silence for a moment. "We have to practice for our final exam," explains Cam, getting into his warm-ups. "It's next week. I guess you won't have to take it."

"Doesn't matter if I take it or not," I say. "I'm leaving right after the show."

"Leaving? What are you talking about?"

"Oh, come on," I say. "It's not like everybody doesn't know I'm a washout. At least give me the courtesy, as ex-friends, not to pretend."

"I don't *believe* you," Jeremy spits out.

"Yeah, well, believe it. You were right from the very first, so feel free to say, *I told you so.* I thought because they picked me, it meant I was ready, that they knew I was ready. They should have picked you instead."

Jeremy gives a harsh laugh. "My mom sure thinks so," he says. Then he sits down beside me. "This is a rough scene, isn't it? Rough on you 'cause you got picked, rough on me 'cause I didn't."

"I heard your mom yelling at you," I admit. "I didn't mean to listen, but I was right there and couldn't help it. She was pretty harsh."

"Yeah, she gets like that. She wants me to be a star. I'm used to it."

"I called my mom. She thinks I *am* a star. From the sounds of it, my entire hometown is coming for what she calls my 'debut.' So I think I can predict that my humiliation will be complete. I almost told her I was going to quit." I sigh. "But I didn't."

Cam smiles. "I can picture it. Sometimes it's hard to get a word in edgewise when your mom gets going." Then he adds, "Which is a good thing, in this case. You can't quit."

"He's right," Jeremy says more seriously. "You know you can't, don't you? Not this close to opening."

"Yeah, I know. Wishful thinking on my part. I won't quit."

"So you'll just do your best," offers Cam. "That's all anybody can ask."

"I don't even know what my best is!" I start pacing back and forth. "Everybody keeps talking at me—do this, do that, try this, try that. I'm so confused, I couldn't even tell you what I'm doing right and what I'm doing wrong! Mr. Acton told us today that the production was flat, that's there's no life, no energy. And it's because of me! I can't make it come together. Do I worry about the choreography, or my technique, or my acting, or whether or not I stay in character? I know for sure I can't do it all, so what do I worry about most?"

"Whoa," says Cam.

"Did Mr. Acton say you had to worry about all that?" asks Jeremy.

"Well, I have to get all those things right, so I guess I have to worry about them all, don't I?"

"What do you do the worst?" asks Cam.

"Gee, thanks for the vote of confidence," I retort.

"Hey, man, you said it, not me. What's hardest?"

"Everything."

The three of us sit there. I don't think they knew how bad it really is.

"Can we help?" asks Jeremy finally.

"Why would you? Apparently, I'm the guy to hate."

"Only because you were being so obnoxious," Jeremy says. "It was kind of a shock that any student got picked. You didn't give us any time to adjust to the news, to understand why they picked you and not us. We would have figured it out. But no, right away it was 'Let me teach you poor slobs all the wonderful things I know because I'm in the company and you're not.'"

Cam cracks up at Jeremy's singsong voice.

"I thought..." I sigh. "Whatever. Was I really that bad?"

Cam grins. "Oh yeah!"

"Make a guy feel better, why don't you?" I groan. "I didn't mean to. But I was so excited, and nobody else was. All of a sudden I was the enemy. It's harsh, losing all your friends at once."

"Aw, we weren't lost," says Cam. "On tour, maybe."

Jeremy snorts.

"Charis says we can't ever really be friends because we have to compete against each other."

"That's stupid," says Jer.

"It's just her barbed wire," adds Cam.

Jer and I stare at him. "Her what?"

"Her barbed wire. Odette's always giving her a hard time, because Charis is the next-best dancer. So Charis has to protect herself, build a shield against Odette, you know? But whenever she's feeling bad, she uses the barbed wire to protect herself from everybody."

My jaw drops. So does Jeremy's. "Thank you, Dr. Cam, for your psychoanalysis," says Jer as he shakes his head. "You know, you are one weird dude."

Cam grins.

There is silence in the change room. I keep pacing. Finally, Cam and Jer look at each other.

"You know what we've got to do, don't you, Jer?" asks Cam.

"No choice," replies Jeremy gravely.

"What?" I ask. "What have you got to do?"

But neither of them answer me. Instead, they leap up from the bench, dump my bag and grab a pair of tights from it, and before I know what's hit me, they've tied me to the pole that's holding up the ceiling of the change room. With my own tights.

"What the heck!" I shout.

"It's time," says Cam.

"For what?" I scream.

Jeremy smiles. "We need to stage an..."

"Intervention!" Cam and Jer high-five each other and run out of the change room, leaving me tied to the pole.

Eleven

I can't believe they've left me like this. I mean, it's ridiculous. I'm busy trying to stretch the tights enough to slide my hands through the knots when the change-room door opens. *Great.*

Mavis giggles. "They weren't kidding!" She laughs again. "They really did tie him up!"

Johanna follows Mavis into the dressing room. "This place is disgusting!" she says, wrinkling her nose. "I'm amazed you don't asphyxiate yourselves with your own BO."

"I don't know what you're doing here, but make yourselves useful and untie me!"

"Hmmm," says Mavis thoughtfully. "No can do. We're under orders."

"What orders?"

"We're not sure yet. But we're not supposed to untie you," replies Johanna. "We're supposed to wait."

"For what?"

The girls shrug their shoulders. Then we sit. I'm still working on the knots when Charis comes in, frowning when she sees me.

"I almost didn't come," she says, "but I'm not like Odette, though you seem to think so."

"Charis, come on," I say. "I didn't mean it. We're friends, remember?"

"I don't know if we're even still *pals*," she retorts as she plunks herself down on the bench.

Next is Sybille. She sees me and bites her lip.

I can't help myself. "Happy now?" I ask.

"I was mad at you. So sue me. You bring out the worst in people, you know, Rob."

"So you being mad at me is all *my* fault?"

Sybille grins. "Yeah. But I'm over it now."

I shake my head. Pretty soon I'm going to need my own barbed wire to protect myself against female logic.

After that we wait, although for what, I have no idea. I'm still working at the knots.

Finally there's a grunt, then a clatter, and Cam and Jeremy drag Odette, literally kicking and screaming, into the change room.

"Get your hands off me! And let me out of here! He is *so* not my problem!"

Jeremy doesn't let her go. He pushes her onto the bench and holds her down.

Who's not her problem? This is not sounding good to me at all.

Cam jumps up onto the bench. "Ladies, we have gathered here today," he intones like an old-time preacher, "to save the Premier Dance Company." Mavis giggles again. "Apparently, Robin here is going to completely ruin the upcoming production. The travesty about to occur is completely and entirely his fault."

"Big surprise," mutters Odette, who is still being held down by Jeremy.

"Gee, thanks, man," I say.

"These tragic words were spoken by the man himself." Cam bows to me with a sweeping arm. "Not for him, but on behalf of the company, we must intervene and save the day."

"Give me a break. And untie me!"

All the girls except for Odette are laughing now.

Cam grabs my copy of the play from the mess of stuff he dumped from my bag. "Only the play can release you." Then he leaps across the room to the other bench. Flipping to the end, he reads from the last act, "*If we shadows have offended...*"

He points at me. "Has he offended?"

"Oh yeah!"

Cam goes back to the book. "*If we have unearnèd luck...* Does he?"

"Oh yeah!"

"What is this, a revival meeting?" I mutter.

"*Give me your hands if we be friends, / And Robin shall restore amends.* Okay, folks, we need to give him a hand!"

There aren't so many "Oh yeahs" after that line.

"Okay, enough," says Jeremy as Cam finally unties me. "This is actually serious. Rob's so frustrated he's about to blow a gasket. Or quit. Whichever comes first. The company's got him all confused, so we have to sort him out. So spill, big guy. Where are you at, and what do you need?"

So I spill.

"I pretty much know the steps now..." I start.

"Well, good for you," says Odette sarcastically. "I mean, you open day after tomorrow."

I ignore her. "The thing is, Rick could really get into character. You really believed he was a fairy. He was light on his feet, and jumpy and playful. And I've tried to copy him, but I can't pull it off. So I've been studying this other Puck off a DVD, and he's more solid—athletic, you know? That works better for me, but I'm not consistent with it."

Johanna says, "Your problem is that you can't channel Puck?"

"Yeah, exactly." I sigh with relief. They get it.

Everybody in the change room bursts out laughing. "He can't channel Puck!" hoots Charis.

"What's funny?"

Jeremy is trying to rearrange his face to look serious, but he's having a hard time. "Here's the thing, Rob. You don't have to channel Puck. You *are* Puck. That's why they picked you."

"I don't get it."

"Think about it. If they'd needed an understudy for Oberon, the King, who would they have picked? Of the three of us, I mean."

Cam answers right away. "You, Jer. You're definitely King material."

"Right," answers Jer firmly. "We're all good dancers, but we're not the same. I'm dignified, stately. Boring." With a quick glance at Sybille, he sighs. "But absolutely solid. What if they'd needed an understudy for Bottom?"

I get it. "Cam, of course. He's funny."

Cam waggles his eyebrows to demonstrate.

"Of course. Cam. He's the comic. But they needed Puck. Explosive, frustrating, disruptive Puck. And you, my man"—Jer punches my arm—"are that guy." For a moment Jeremy looks sad. "Even if my mother doesn't get it."

"What you need to do," Charis goes on, "is the same stuff you do in class with us. Play games, tease. Be a smart aleck. You don't want to make people laugh, like Bottom does. You want them to feel like strangling you, even though they love you because you're so clever."

"Yeah," adds Sybille. "Just be you." At that, everybody breaks up again.

Everybody except Odette. "It's not funny," she huffs, and then she looks straight at me. "And I won't help you. You're not a serious dancer—you'd rather mess things up to get a laugh. It's no surprise to me that you fall apart when things get a little tough." With that, she shrugs off Jeremy's hold and marches to the door. Then she turns and casts her evil eye on everybody else. "Why would you even bother to help him?"

"Because sometimes dancers have to work as a team," Charis shoots back. "And this is one of those times. If you're not going to help, make sure you close the door on your way out."

"Help *you*? No way." Odette's glare hones in on me again. "For the record, I think strangling him sounds like a much better idea." And with that, she's out the door.

"Wow," says Mavis. "That was a little harsh."

I shrug. "I don't care what she thinks. I care what you guys think. So how do I just be me onstage?"

I pace while everybody thinks. "For starters, you have to stop copying other Pucks," says Charis. "You have to be your own Puck."

"But how do I create my own Puck?"

Everybody thinks some more.

"It's obvious, isn't it?" asks Cam. "You have to prank the other dancers."

"Prank the company?" Sybille looks horrified. "He can't do that."

"Sybille's right," I say. "It's the company, not you guys!" Charis glares at me. "Okay, sorry—

I didn't mean it like that. But these guys are stars!"

"All the more reason," says Cam. "You, my man," he goes on, poking me in the chest, "are intimidated by them."

"Well, yeah. Aren't you?"

"Of course," says Cam. "But I don't have to dance with them. You do. Am I right, or am I right, Jer?"

Jeremy has gone a little green, which makes me laugh.

"You're right," he says, "but the very idea of pranking the company makes me feel sick to my stomach."

"So what's the prank?" asks Mavis. "What will you do?"

"Here," says Cam. He throws my copy of the play at me. "Read it again. You'll figure something out."

I feel the old magic coming back. Pranking magic. "Jer, can I borrow Ratinski?"

As the girls squeal, Jeremy slumps down. "Please, please," he whispers to himself. "Please don't let my mother find out."

Twelve

I lay awake all night, leafing back and forth through the play. Cam's right—it's all in here. Puck frightens the maidens of the village, misleads night wanderers, changes into a horse and later a hog...but that's all kind of difficult to reproduce onstage. Especially that bit about changing into a crab apple, although how cool would it be to bob about as an apple in somebody's drink, then change back into a miniature fairy to scare the bejeezus out of them as they took a drink? But I can definitely make things go missing and knock people down. All Puck really does is make everybody mad, then make it all better. I can do that.

The fact that the company dancers don't really know me is in my favor. They won't be expecting a sneak attack. But Cam was right. I do feel intimidated by them. Is pranking the company going to make that better? Or much, much worse?

At breakfast I'm still thinking so hard about the whole idea that I don't hear my name being called, and Mr. Colson has to come right to my table and tap me on the shoulder. "Mr. Acton wants to see you in his office, Robin," he says quietly. He looks serious.

Shoot. Maybe it's too late. I have to drag myself down the hallway.

"Come in, Robin," says Mr. Acton. "Sit down."

Here it comes.

"I'm going to have to replace you as Puck. I'm sorry, Robin, but I'm really worried about the performance. So is the rest of the company. I'm afraid we may have made a mistake assigning such an important role to a student."

"You couldn't know that Rick would break his ankle." It's all I can think to say.

"True," says Mr. Acton, "but that's the point of an understudy, and I know better than to assume accidents won't happen. Please don't think I'm disappointed in you. It was my mistake for putting too much on your shoulders too soon. I hope you won't feel bad about being replaced, but I don't see that I have any choice. You'll have other chances."

Not feel bad? While I wait for other chances? We both know they won't be coming my way. It's now or never.

"Mr. Acton, I have an idea. Please, will you give me one more chance?"

"Robin, I applaud your dedication. No one could have worked harder. But the dress rehearsal is this afternoon! There's no time left for more chances."

"At least listen to my idea. Please?" And I tell him. At first he just looks tired and a little impatient. Then I see it—the smallest twitch on one side of his mouth. I know he wants to laugh— I know it! Not many would notice, but true pranksters recognize each other. So I embellish, add layers. His eyes crinkle. It's working.

When I finally run out of breath, Mr. Acton sits back in his chair and crosses his arms. "You know the company dancers may never speak to you again, don't you?"

"As long as they'll dance with me, I won't care," I say firmly.

"Humph," he snorts. I sit on the edge of my seat as he thinks. "You could use Starveling's lantern." Then he grins. *He's in!* And so am I, for one more rehearsal, at least.

This is going to have to be epic.

* * *

"You have got to be kidding me, man," Cam says. "Are you really going to wear this? Or *not* wear this?" He and Jer are helping me into my costume, such as it is. It'll leave me about as close to dancing naked as you can be without getting arrested.

"What can I say?" I try to sound breezy. "Fairies are supposed to be like spirits or something. Since when did spirits wear clothes?"

"True," says Jeremy skeptically. "But I think wrapping yourself in fig leaves went out with Adam and Eve. As a fashion statement, this is a little out there, you know."

I look in the mirror. The silk vine wraps around me, and as far as I can tell, it covers everything that needs to be covered. Barely. "So shoot the costume designer. I've got enough to worry about."

But here's the thing. My mother is going to see me in this. So yeah, I'm worried.

"Have you got it all set up?" asks Cam. He and Jer cut school this morning to go to the joke shop downtown for me. I had a long shopping list for them, and they didn't miss a single item.

"I skipped lunch to get everything ready, so we're good," I reply. "Where are you sitting?"

"Front row, center," says Cam. "That way I'll be able to see everything."

"I'm going to be backstage, stage right. I'll have to hide until I can collect Ratinski," adds Jeremy. "Then, of course, I'll have to run for my life." He groans. "How is it I always get talked into this stuff?" He shakes his head in frustration.

"Because you're a good guy." I slap him on the shoulder. "Remember, this is for the good of the company, right? We're going to save the show. Anyway," I add, "Charis is going to distract your mother until it's all over. And you know Charis. Your mom's not getting anywhere near this theater until she says so, dress rehearsal or not."

"I can only hope," mutters Jer.

Right then Charis walks in. "Jeremy, I told your mom that Mr. Acton wanted some changes to the program, so she's down in the office. It'll keep her there for a while." She eyes me up and down. "He didn't really want changes, so I had to fake it. I rewrote your bio, Rob. You're now a mechanical robot designed in a lab to be a perfect dancer. But there were so many errors in your software, they threw you away. Unfortunately, we got stuck with you. Hope you don't mind. I think it reads well."

"You're so amusing."

"Love the horns," she adds.

"What can I say? In some cultures, Puck is considered a demon."

"My, my." Charis grins from ear to ear. "Robin Goodman, I do believe you've found the perfect role!"

"Ha-ha."

"And they go so well with...whatever it is you're not wearing. When you said you wanted girls to go for you because of your body, we didn't realize you were going to put it all out there. Can we auction you off after the show?"

Cam chortles. "We told him, but he insists on wearing it."

"You guys are all so very hilarious. Wish me luck," I say as I go into the rehearsal studio to warm up.

"Yeah," they say. "Break a leg, why doncha?"

"Sorry," I call back. "It's been done."

When I walk into the studio, I get a few surprised looks and a lot of frowns. I guess the company didn't expect me back. I take a deep breath. Well, I'm here, and I'm staying. I go to the barre and close my eyes. As I run through the warm-up, I imagine Puck inside of me. My Puck, nobody else's.

He makes me feel like I want to jump out of my body.

"Hang on, Puck," I whisper to myself. "It's nearly time."

*　　*　　*

As I wait in the wings, I think of one thing and one thing only. Not the steps. Not the jumps. Not the havoc about to come. I think about pinball. The old-fashioned kind. The kind with the flappers and the little silver ball that pings all around, bouncing off obstacles whenever it hits something. That pinball is me. I am a ball of energy, waiting to be released. And when I go, I'm going to fly around the stage, pinging everything in my path. Ping, ping, ping...the music builds, and I'm off!

As I leap into the spotlight, my grand jeté feels like an explosion. Once I'm on, I have a short solo and then usually hide behind a tree. But today, I chase Peaseblossom, confusing her. Then I hide behind her skirt. This is the dress rehearsal, and she can't react, or call time, but I can feel her confusion. She's watching me now. I tug on her skirt as I peek around her at the audience. She looks down and tries to catch my eye so I can see her glare, but I don't look. I sure can feel it though. Then I crawl between her legs and lift her up so she's sitting on me, and she shrieks. As she settles on my back, I buck and knock her off. I'm gentle about it, but the fact is, Puck turning into a stool is actually in the play. So it's a legit move. I just hadn't thought of really studying the words until Cam's little performance in the change room last night. I jump up and bow to

Peaseblossom with what I hope looks like a cheeky grin, then run before she can hit me. One down, literally.

In the next act, Bottom asks Peter Quince to unroll his scroll and read the players' names. With great fanfare, Quince slowly unrolls the massive scroll. I angle toward upstage center so I can hear Cam. I know he's going to laugh. As Quince gets to the end of the scroll, the whole thing bursts open and streamers explode from it. Quince drops it as if it were a snake, then jumps away and stares at the mess on the floor. I love it! And Cam is killing himself. I have to make sure they know it was me, so I pick up the streamers and, with great deference, arrange them on Quince's head. Then I step back to admire my work. None of this is in the script, but this is dress rehearsal, right? It's like filming live—you have to go with what you've got. Quince looks like a thundercloud, but Bottom is starting to grin. *Just wait, Bottom, your turn is next!*

It's been a long time since I clubbed Bottom with the donkey head. I think he's suspicious that something like that is going to happen, and from the back I can see his shoulders tighten in anticipation. But no, the donkey head makes it safely onto his head. What he doesn't know is that I've given it a new look. There's a beard, and a long mustache, and I've added gigantic false eyelashes, a golden wig and a silver tiara. Bottom can't see it, so he doesn't know why he's hearing snickers from the other dancers, snickers they're trying hard to conceal from the audience. Snickers are good, but what I really want is a big laugh, one the dancers can't contain.

Oberon is up next. He's supposed to go stage left and pick the magical purple flower, then give it to me so I can cast the love spell. Oberon does his stately dance across the stage and reaches down for the flower. But it's not there. He looks again. Nothing. If his character was supposed to be comical, he could play it up, but Oberon is the King. It's hard to look dignified when everybody knows you've been suckered. For the sake of the music—we can't get too far behind—I dance sweetly over to him and hand him the missing flower. Then he hands it right back, which, of course, looks ridiculous. More snickers. A couple of lesser fairies pick up other, smaller flowers from around the stage and hand them solemnly to Oberon, making him even more disconcerted. That's not supposed to happen.

Now I have allies. The other fairies cover for me as more props go missing, and I'm never where they expect me to be. Unbelievably, we keep up with the music and the plot proceeds as it should, in spite of my unscheduled disruptions. There's only one prank left to go.

From stage left comes Starveling, carrying his lantern. He's supposed to think the lantern is the moon, and that he's the man in the moon. When he gets to center stage, he stops and opens the little door in the lantern so that the light can shine out. But this time, there is no light. Instead, there's Ratinski, happily chewing a hunk of cheese inside the lantern. Starveling shrieks and throws the lantern away from him. I'm ready for it (Jeremy made me swear Ratinski wouldn't get hurt), so I catch the lantern as it falls. Meanwhile, Starveling backs into Bottom, who can't really see very well under the donkey's head. They both fall down, and while the other characters are trying to help them up, I bring the lantern back into the crowd of fairies, and the shrieking starts up all over again. It's a wonderful, fantastic, messy tangle, and if I hadn't promised Jeremy I wouldn't, I'd be tempted to let the rat out of the lantern and really have some fun. But for Ratinski's sake, I'd better not.

The dancers manage to untangle themselves and get back to the performance, and I hand off the lantern to Jeremy, waiting in the wings. He looks like he's in shock. There's a lot of improv going on as the dancers find their places in the choreography. I bet a lot of companies couldn't get back on track after something like that. But the Premier Dance Company can do anything. I play it cool for the rest of the production, right to the very last moment when the artificial fog rolls across the stage, making us all disappear as the curtain finally drops.

I'm mobbed. I don't know if they're going to kiss me or kill me, but I'm not worried. I did what I had to do. If they didn't like it, if they're mad, if it wasn't enough to keep the role, well, that's the way it goes. But at least I tried.

Thirteen

Cam and Jer catch me in the hall and pull me into a small studio. "That was awesome, man!" Cam says.

"Thanks! You know I couldn't have done it without you, right?"

"The look on Quince's face! It was priceless!" Jer exclaims.

"Yeah, and when you decorated his hair with the streamers? He couldn't believe it was happening!" Cam doubles up with laughter.

"The one I really liked was when Oberon couldn't find the flower. He was trying so hard to be kingly, but up close you could tell that he was saying, *What the hell?*" Jer casts his eyes skyward and sighs. "It was beautiful."

I don't say much. It's more fun to listen to them do a postmortem on the prank. But much as I want the moment to last, duty calls.

"I gotta go," I say. "Mr. Acton's called an immediate debriefing."

Cam laughs. "You think? This debrief will be historic!"

"What do you think they'll do to you?" asks Jer in a worried voice. "I mean, the rest of the dancers have got to be mad."

"All I know is that they can't make me feel any worse than I felt before I did it," I say. "So... whatever. I'll roll with it." I take a deep breath and go into the studio.

*   *   *

"What he did was insane! He threw everything off!"

"I thought I'd throw up, I laughed so hard!"

"Bellamy, you can't let him get away with this!"

"Bottom, I really like your new look..."

"Now the show is going to be totally ruined!"

"Quiet! Be quiet!"

It takes a long minute for everybody to shut up. Mr. Acton, Mr. Colson and Miss Amelia are all standing at the front of the large rehearsal studio. Finally, there is quiet.

"So," says Mr. Acton in a calm voice, "are you all awake now?"

The company dancers frown and look at one another.

"Yes, awake. Yesterday this production was on life support. Today there's enough energy in this room to start a nuclear reaction. I'd say I prefer the latter, although something in between would be even better."

Nobody speaks.

"We blamed Puck for not being good enough, but it's Puck who figured out how to pull this piece together. Don't any of you forget that." Mr. Acton takes in every single one of us in his stare. "That said, today was a once-only. A wake-up call. Now we need to channel all this energy and get to work. Titania, in Act 1 I need you to..."

It's the most intense debrief I've ever been in. Mr. Acton goes through every step, every phrase, every character. Inevitably, he gets to me.

"Robin, let's keep the bucking stool—it works with your character. But I noticed that in all the confusion, you left out your final double tour. Don't let that happen again."

"No, sir," I reply smartly. But inside I groan. I knew he'd notice, but I was hoping he'd say the ending looked better without it. Fat chance. As we all finally leave the studio to go to dinner, I get shoulder punches and back thumps from the other dancers. I'm in, but I'm not done.

I now have just one day to master that stupid jump, so right after dinner it's back to the studio for me. I've been at it for about half an hour when I see a shadow pass by the door, then back up. Someone peeks in. I groan. Odette. And she's coming inside. Just what I need.

"What are you doing here?" Odette frowns.

"What does it look like? I'm practicing."

"Why?" asks Odette. She actually looks confused.

"What's so weird about practicing? You do it all the time." I wish she'd go.

"Yeah, but I'm a dancer. You're an idiot." She sniffs, turns to go, then whirls back. "That, that...circus you caused today? It was disgusting.

Not that you care, but somebody could have been hurt. And it looked ridiculous."

"I'm hardly going to do that in performance. Not even you could believe that," I shoot back. "It was...necessary. A step in the process. I cleared it with Mr. Acton first, you know. I'm not a complete idiot, much as you would like to think so."

That surprises her. "Mr. Acton actually *let* you do that?" she asks.

I sigh. Why doesn't she go away? "Look, if you must know, rehearsal wasn't going well. Yeah, yeah, just as you predicted. So you were right. And I was a mess. We thought it would help."

Odette stares at me. "So why are you here? Practicing?" She makes it sound like a dirty word. "If Mr. Acton likes the fact that you're an idiot, why bother practicing?"

"Will you cut it out with the idiot business?" I'm practically yelling now. "Here's the thing. This was supposed to be my big break. I wanted to do it right, okay? So I stopped fooling around, and look where that got me. I always thought I was a pretty good dancer, but if you take away the fooling around, it turns out I'm not as good as I thought I was. Not good enough for the company anyway. So I have to practice. Happy?"

"Ah, he finally sees the light," Odette says sarcastically. Then she frowns and turns to go. She looks kind of sad.

"What?" I say. "What's the matter?"

Odette sighs. "At least you have something unique. You're a dancer *and* an idiot. I'm just a dancer. If my rehearsal didn't go well, I wouldn't have anything to add to the mix. Only technique, and if it doesn't measure up, I've got nothing."

Oh boy. Where is Dr. Cam, psychoanalyst—heavy on the *psycho*—when you need him? What do I say?

"Ummm..."

"Don't even try, Rob! Don't think this is true confessions or anything, because it's not. It's reality. I have to be the best, because technique is all I've got. Charis has passion, Sybille's romantic, and Johanna can do young and innocent. Mavis plays the comic. Everybody else has this other layer, but I just dance."

"Maybe you have another layer but haven't found it yet?" I suggest weakly.

"Oh, shut up," Odette says fiercely. "Your balance is wrong on the double tour—that's why you can't do it, you know. That's what you're practicing, right? Watch me."

Odette pulls off her sweats, does a couple of stretches, then faces me. Feet in fifth position, plié, then...she flies straight up in a perfect double tour.

"How did you do that?" I ask, aghast. "Girls don't do double tours!"

"Like guys don't dance on pointe, right? Except when they do. You're being an idiot again, Rob." She prepares, then does a second perfect double tour.

I want to cry.

"I'm a dancer," she says. "I can do any step I want." She crosses the floor, grabs my arm and drags me to center. "You're a mover."

I groan.

"Nothing wrong with that. When you're moving straight and fast, you eat up the floor. Your problem is when you try to turn. Think about it. What are your best moves?"

"Grand jeté, cabriole..."

"Yeah, the steps that move you full steam straight ahead. What are your worst?"

"Well, double tour, of course..." I think about it. "And pirouettes."

"Right," she says firmly. "All the moves that require rotation. Whenever you try to turn, your brain gets twisted. Your idiot side tries to get creative or something, I don't know. And it means you miss the most important part of the whole jump."

"What's that?" I ask suspiciously.

"The snap. Watch me again." Fifth position, plié, and she's soaring.

Then she looks at me. "Did you hear it?"

"Hear what?"

Odette sighs.

Maybe I really am an idiot, because I haven't the faintest idea what she's talking about. I watch her go to the desk and tear a sheet of paper off a pad. She sticks one corner of the paper under the leg elastic of her leotard so that it dangles down between her thighs. Then she goes to the middle of the floor, takes fifth position again, pliés and shoots into the air. What sounds like a shot rings out as her thighs slap together. I jump and she says, "So *now* did you hear it?"

"That was amazing!" I'm still trying to get my heart rate down.

"That's the snap. It's your thighs that hold you up straight." Odette looks smug. I pick the paper up off the floor. It's practically torn in two.

"Try it," she orders.

This is just plain wacky, but I take fifth position, plié, then fly straight up, rotating as I snap my thighs and think of gunshot wounds. And I do a perfect double tour.

"What the...?"

"Again!"

I do it again. Perfect again. I don't believe this.

"Keep practicing," Odette says. "And don't forget that you're still an idiot."

An idiot who's in total shock, and I'm not the only one. The door opens and Charis comes in, looking seriously surprised.

"What are you doing here?" she demands.

I open my mouth, but she's not asking me.

"That stunt this afternoon only got him halfway there. He still has to actually dance," Odette replies, "and he'll kill the reputation of the school if he flubs the very last move. Somebody had to deal with it."

"So you're helping him? Really?"

"You're not the only one who cares about the company, Charis."

"Ladies?" I seem to have become invisible again.

"But you *hate* Robin."

"How do you know how I feel?"

"Ladies?"

They both turn my way, looking a little startled. *Ha!* So I really did become invisible. Talk about channeling Puck.

"Can he actually do it?" Charis looks questioningly at Odette, who nods.

"Let me see," Charis demands.

I look over at Odette as she says, "Remember the snap." I nod.

Feet in fifth position, plié, and then I fly straight up in a perfect double tour. "Third in a row," I say, grinning.

"You are some teacher!" Charis says, looking at Odette with disbelief.

"Don't I get any credit?" I ask.

"No," both girls answer at once.

Fourteen

I've been in lots of shows before, but never as part of a professional company. There's a different vibe. Every dancer knows they're going to push themselves to the limit, because that's what we do for the audience. So there's an air of seriousness and intense focus.

That is, until a runner knocks on the door. He's ushered into the change room, carrying an enormous bouquet of red roses.

"For Robin Goodman," he squeaks out. There are titters all around. I want to either die or kill my mother, whichever comes first. Only principals get flowers. I have no choice but to take them, but having done that, I don't know what to do with them.

Peaseblossom saunters over with a vase. "From your mommy?" she asks sweetly.

"She used to be my mom," I reply grimly. "She's just been disowned."

That gets a laugh. I sigh. I stick the bouquet into the vase, then reconsider. Taking the flowers back, I pull out one long-stemmed rose and present it to Peaseblossom.

"For the ten little bruises," I say.

Peaseblossom goes red. "I didn't really have bruises."

"I know." I grin. Then I make my way around the room, handing roses to all the ladies. They're all shaking their heads at this lame performance, but at least I'm getting rid of the flowers. Finally, there's only one left. I go up to Oberon.

"Just in case you can't find the flower tonight," I say as I present him with the rose. The whole room breaks up at the look on the King's face.

"Gotcha!" I laugh. And the beauty of it is, they really don't know what I'm going to do tonight. Anything could happen.

* * *

When the orchestra stops tuning its instruments, the lights dim and the buzz from the audience quiets. This is it. *Own the stage.* That's what they tell you. My grand jeté takes me front and center, and I know the stage is mine. But not only mine. As I do my short solo, I can feel every other dancer onstage. They're watching me, waiting to react if I do something crazy. I won't, of course, not in performance, but now I wonder if somebody else will. We're all on high alert, watching one another, waiting for the opportunity to play up the gags.

Peaseblossom gets me first. When I pretend to be the three-legged stool and she sits on me, she smiles sweetly, then tickles me under cover of her skirt. I buck her off two beats early, because if I don't, I'll bust out laughing. Not cool. From the looks on the faces of the nearby fairies, they were in on it, so I use my two counts to tickle the one closest to me. That gets them going, and for the next eight counts, we're all grinning like crazy. We're supposed to smile, but this is coming naturally, which makes it way more fun.

Oberon's flower is where it's supposed to be, but when he hands it to me, I see the red rose tucked inside the big purple blossom. He gives me a kingly smile, then winks. I swear I leap higher as I dance offstage to make the love potion.

Peter Quince struts when he reads from the scroll. I didn't pack it with streamers this time, which he no doubt has already checked, but the strut tells us all that he's on top of it. The audience cracks up when they see that Bottom has decided to keep the tiara on the donkey head, and there's a breathless moment onstage just before Starveling opens his lantern. Ratinski's not there, of course, but there *is* a rat. It takes a second for the other dancers to realize that Starveling has stuck a small stuffed rat into the pocket of his costume to honor the memory. I know to look for it, because, well, who do you think he got the stuffed rat from? The inside joke ramps up the energy even more. We are so *on*. It feels amazing.

The energy keeps on building as the dance draws to a close. For everybody but me, that is. My high starts to leak away as the double tour gets closer and closer. I tense up and nearly miss a step. Luckily, I'm supposed to hide behind a tree right after, so I have a chance to catch my breath and get my head straight. *Focus, Robin!*

That's when I see Odette. She was assigned backstage duties, so she's been around all night, helping with costumes and props and stuff, but now she's in the wings. She's really not supposed to be there, and she never breaks rules, so I keep half an eye on her as she unclips a piece of paper from her clipboard. Then she looks straight at me and very deliberately waves the piece of paper in front of her face.

The snap.

I have twelve more counts to think about the jump. Then I leap out from behind the tree. It's the last scene of the whole dance, and everybody is looking at me. It's Puck's job—no, *my* job—to bring the whole dance—every dancer, every step, every beat of the music—to a satisfactory close. No pressure.

Feet in fifth position, plié, and then I fly straight up, rotating as I go. Twice. Energy shoots from my toes upward, and I'm flying, I'm turning...

Snap.

It's a blur after that. The stage manager must have flicked the switch that makes the fog roll out over the stage, because I can feel myself disappearing from sight. I know the lights grow dim, the curtains close and the music goes quiet, but it all feels like a dream.

Only for five seconds, of course. Then I hear applause, and the rest of the dancers are pouring back onto the stage for our bow. I take my place in line. *Give me your hands if we be friends.* Together we lift our joined hands in the air and bow to the audience.

Fifteen

Mr. Acton is pleased. Not overjoyed but pleased.

"I liked the feeling onstage tonight," he says. "Light and fun but with an edge. Good work, everyone. We'll debrief tomorrow morning at nine. For now, your public awaits!" Everybody backstage claps, and Mr. Acton grins, bowing with a grand flourish.

"We were way better tonight than I thought we'd be," says Peaseblossom. "Even you." She grins, poking me good-naturedly.

The fairies joke with Starveling about his rat, and Bottom and Titania work out a hitch in Act 4. "I still haven't got the timing quite right in that middle section," mutters Peter Quince. It's interesting to hear the company dancers parse their performances, but right now I don't even care. I did it!

Oberon taps me on the shoulder. "For you," he says, bowing low. He gives me back my rose, and everybody bursts out laughing.

Then Rick bursts through the dressing-room door—literally. His wheelchair practically takes out the doorjamb. "It was great! I went incognito in the audience, and the vibe was good. They really got the fact that it was all a dream. And you, kid"—he wheels around to face me—"that was a mean double tour you managed out there. You were holding out on us!"

We're supposed to stay in our costumes and hit the lobby as a group, but first we have to mop up sweat and freshen our makeup so we're not too gross to mingle with polite company. As I wait for the others to be ready, I spot Odette and head her way.

"Hey," I say.

"Hey yourself."

"What did you think?" I don't know why I'm nervous asking.

"For a guy who just learned the jump last night," she says, "it wasn't too bad." She has her odious voice on, but I think I can hear a hint of a smile.

"Come on, Robin, we're ready," calls Peaseblossom.

"I have to go. Odette?"

"Yeah?"

"We're having pizza tonight to kill time until the reviews come out. Do you want to come?"

"Pizza? You've got to be kidding."

"I like pizza. So shoot me."

She hesitates.

"In the kitchen, kind of a midnight raid, so we can have ice cream after the pizza."

"Ice cream? Gross!" She stalks away.

* * *

Walking out into the lobby as a company member—well, I can't describe it. There are squeals and shouts of "There they are!" and we're mobbed. The principals are anyway. Me, well, I am too, but my mob consists mostly of my family and the better part of my hometown.

"Robin!" My mother literally shrieks my name as she runs across the lobby toward me, spreading her arms wide for a hug. It's like a bad car commercial. "You were spectacular, the best in the whole show!" *Ouch. Say that a little louder, why don't you, Mom?*

I brace myself for the hug. "Hi, Mom." As the life is squeezed out of me, I catch sight of Jeremy standing with his mom as she chats up a big donor. He grins at me. Moms will be moms, I guess. Dad's turn comes next, and my brothers do the man-hug thing, then my cousins and Aunt Sally and Uncle Harry, and after that I kind of lose the names. Everybody's talking at once, and I let it roll over me until Mom's voice rises above the chatter.

"But really, darling, that costume? Don't you think that's a little inappropriate?"

I swear every single person milling about in the lobby stops mingling and stares at me. All of me. About every inch of me that it is possible to stare at. I sigh.

"Yeah, man," says my oldest brother. "What can I say? You've sure got balls to wear something like that out in public."

"One wrong move and we'll be able to see the balls in question!" my other brother adds, laughing. "You better stop that leaping around, bro."

I lean in so the three of us are head to head. "Take a look around," I say. Their eyes widen when they see what I knew they were going to see. All eyes are on me, all right, including those of every hottie in the place.

"Whoa," says my oldest brother. "Chick magnet."

"Want to borrow it sometime?" I ask.

*   *   *

Mom wants to do this whole party thing at the swanky hotel, but I beg off until breakfast with the promise that I'll bring Cam and Jeremy with me. It's one last hug, and then Dad and my brothers corral Mom and point her toward the door. I mouth a big *thank-you* to them as they head out the door. I think she's still talking sequins.

I stay and mingle with the company for a while, but they don't party on opening night, I guess because of that nine o'clock debriefing and all. I'm too keyed up to go to bed, so while I change, Charis, Sybille, Johanna and Mavis steal the key to the kitchen and Cam and Jeremy order the pizza. That'll keep us going until the reviews come out—online first, and then the media start printing hard copies for the morning newspaper delivery. I get to the kitchen as Cam and Jer arrive with the pizza, and a moment later Odette shows up. I didn't think she'd come, but I'm nowhere near as surprised as everybody else.

"Odette," says Jeremy. "Ah, hi."

"Hi."

"Come on in," says Charis. Johanna stares at her as if to say, *Are you kidding?* Sybille's frowning.

"Yeah, Odette, pizza's here," I say. "You need to celebrate your great success."

"What success?" asks Mavis. "What are you talking about?"

"You did take note of my absolutely brilliant double tour tonight?"

Cam grins. "No, actually," he says. "We couldn't bear to watch, so we all had our eyes closed."

"Ha-ha," I reply. "Odette taught me how to do it."

"No way," says Jeremy.

"I was there," says Charis with a shrug. "Saw it with my own eyes."

"Well, somebody had to do *something*," replies Odette, with just a trace of odious. "I couldn't let him embarrass us."

"So in honor of this miracle," I say, "I have a gift."

Odette frowns, and everybody else looks puzzled.

"My mom sent me flowers," I go on. There are commiserating groans all around.

"Like in Baby Ballet," Jeremy says, chortling, "when every kid is the star of the show."

"Yeah, well, what can you do?" I say. "I gave them away."

"Good move," says Cam. "You don't want to be caught dead with flowers."

"Yeah, all but one," I reply. With a flourish, I present it to Odette. "For your hitherto unknown teaching skills."

For a minute I think she won't take it. Her eyes begin to flare into that omnipresent glare. Then she stops. She takes the rose, and she smiles. Honest to goodness, she actually smiles. There are catcalls all around.

*   *   *

"I can't believe you eat this junk," says Odette, wrinkling her nose at the smell of grease.

"It's a myth that dancers don't eat pizza," Cam retorts. "Do you really want to be the one who proves the stereotype true?"

Everybody bursts out laughing. "Don't worry," Cam continues. "We truly appreciate your efforts to uphold the cliché on our behalf, and we love you for it."

"It's not only me!" Odette insists as she turns red. "Jeremy comes from a proper ballet background, and he's not eating pizza!"

So Jeremy locks eyes with Odette and reaches for a piece of pizza. Slowly, slowly, he raises it to his mouth, then stuffs practically the whole piece in. With great huge bites he demolishes it, spraying bits of mushroom and olive all over the table. The girls groan, and Cam and I howl.

"You are *so* disgusting," says Odette primly. Then she delicately reaches for a slice, and we laugh even harder.

"Well," says Sybille, looking at me as she wipes her fingers, "you weren't Rick, but you weren't bad." I throw a napkin at her.

"So he's still your heartthrob?" Johanna asks. "I don't want to be nosy, I just want to keep up." Everybody laughs.

"I'm so over him," says Sybille firmly, as if we all should have been able to guess. "It wouldn't work to have a boyfriend in the company anyway."

We all hoot. "Finally, she sees the light!" I say.

"So who will it be now?" asks Charis. "Inquiring minds want to know."

"Oh, I don't know," Sybille says airily. Then she takes the napkin I threw at her and dabs some of the tomato sauce off Jeremy's face. He practically melts.

Cam's eyes grow big, and he shakes his head in wonder. "What a night!"

*   *   *

Mavis is surfing the Net, jumping from one critic's site to the next to see who will post first. Suddenly she yelps.

"Here it is!" she cries. "Mamie Blue from the *Gazette*!"

We all crowd around the screen.

"*With Noah Grayson and Rick Mathews on the injury list, expectations were that the Premier Dance Company's* A Midsummer Night's Dream *would be nothing more than a placeholder, a lighthearted, easy romp for the less-experienced dancers,"* Mavis reads. *"It was indeed lighthearted, but there were a few moments of note."*

"What moments? Whose moments? Does she mention me?" I can't help myself.

"Hang on, hang on," says Mavis, scrolling down the page.

"Yes!" she shouts. "Here you are!"

"Robin Goodman as Puck had particularly big shoes to fill. Only sixteen and still a student, he stepped into Rick Mathews's role just one week before opening night. Although lacking in strength and maturity, his lively interpretation of Puck amused and satisfied. Brash, merry, yet unsettling, Goodman became 'that shrewd and knavish sprite' in body and spirit, a characterization that clearly galvanized his fellow dancers. Certainly his performance suggests that the Premier Dance Company has depth within its ranks and a strong future ahead of it."

"Wow," says Charis. "That's awesome."

"Lacking in strength and maturity is awesome?" I groan. "Since when?"

"A *lively interpretation* that *amused and satisfied* is pretty darn good," says Jer. *"Galvanized his fellow dancers*? I sure wouldn't mind somebody saying that about my work."

"And anyway," Cam adds, "you're supposed to lack strength and maturity. You're sixteen. We're all sixteen. We have to totally embrace our immaturity for as long as possible."

Charis and Johanna jump him, beating him about the head, and Cam is laughing so hard he can't get away. Jer jumps in, and it's a free-for-all. I'm about to prove how immature I can be when I see that Odette is starting to look a little odious again. She rolls her eyes and stands up, and I'm sure she's going to leave. Wrong again. "Ice cream?" she asks me.

All I can do is stare. Of all the surprises—my big break, the epic prank, Jer and Sybille, the double tour—watching Odette eat ice cream may be the biggest shock of all.

"Sure," I reply. "I could do ice cream."

Acknowledgments

I would like to thank the teachers of the world—all the teachers who have explained, encouraged, inspired, cajoled, disciplined, handed out gold stars and, quite simply, believed in us. We are better people for them. In particular, my thanks go out to the dance teachers who have touched my family: Miss Celeste, Madame Van der Post, Gina Sinclair, Arabella Martin, Lynn Spargo, Maureen Eastick and Lynda Raino. To Clinton and Ashley, thank you for bringing dance home I loved every recital and still smile when I find errant sequins stuck to the floor. Thanks so much to Orca for helping to celebrate the arts, and to my editor, Robin Stevenson. It's been a pleasure. And, as always, thanks to Dale.

PENNY DRAPER is the award-winning author of numerous books for kids and teens. She lives in Victoria, British Columbia, and when she isn't writing, can often be found zooming around on her motorbike or standing on her head in yoga class. Before Penny started writing books, she told stories orally, working for many years as a professional storyteller. She shared tales at schools, libraries, festivals, on radio and television and once from inside a bear's belly. For more information, visit www.pennydraper.ca.

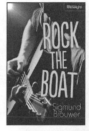